ImPeRfEcT iNsiDe

By

SCOTT M SULLIVAN

www.SullivanAuthor.com

ISBN-13: 978-0-9904823-3-8
ISBN-10: 0990482332

Also by
Scott M Sullivan

THE TRINITY SIGNS
IMPETUS

** AUTHOR'S NOTE **

This fictional novel deals with the powerful disease of depression, and its negative ramifications in everyday life. The story and characters within the book's pages are completely fictional. The emotions and power of the disease, however, are quite real, and gleaned from various sufferers. It would be naïve to think that depression can be cured in a manner put forth in Imperfect Inside; it's simply not realistic. That is what fiction's about, though: sending you on a journey, making you think, or simply providing entertainment.

If you know of someone suffering from depression, be kind and supportive to them. Sometimes a little can mean a lot.

In the USA, the National Suicide Prevention Hotline is: 1-800-273-8255

1

I stared blankly at the finger-smudged monitor on my desk, counting down the minutes until I could stealthily sneak away from my cubicle. A severe hangover wouldn't allow me to do much more than that. I closed my eyes and tried to ignore the noise around me.

"Excuse me, Sean."

Fuck.

Startled, I looked over my shoulder.

When one of the lemmings I worked with was daring enough to enter my cubicle-coffin, it was with trepidation and an uneasy feeling that was palpable. Betty was no different. I could see it on her face. She didn't want to talk to me anymore than I wanted to talk to her. But there we were, looking disdainfully at one another, at an unspoken impasse that only I knew existed.

Betty's large, fawn-like eyes conveyed a sense of helplessness that I'd seen a million times before. She stood there in her overly-yellow dress, with bright pink straps, like an Easter candy gone horribly awry. She waited with her brow raised and her attitude brewing. She undoubtedly had a technical problem.

Why else would she be in front of me? But Betty picked the wrong day to ask for help. I could barely focus, let alone think.

"Sorry to bother you," Betty said, "but my mouse is acting funny." She held the wireless mouse upside down in her hand as if she was about to eulogize it. Its blinking red light was a sure sign that all it needed was fresh batteries.

It was those kinds of mundane and pointless tech questions that I'd get daily; questions that could have been solved with even a millisecond of rational thought. But why would they want to think for themselves when they had me to do it for them?

"Did you put in a helpdesk ticket?" I asked.

"No," she said. "I figured it would be easy, so I didn't bother."

"Fix it yourself if it's so damn easy." That's what I wanted to say. But I didn't. Instead, I said, "You know the process, Betty."

If I had given into the temptation to be mean, it would have led to a longer conversation than I wanted to have. Betty was okay in my book. She was a genuinely nice person who didn't bother me all that much. But I didn't want to hear about her bratty kids, whatever their names were, or how her husband also "works with computers." No offense, Betty, but being a cashier at Shopper's World wasn't exactly "working with computers." Plus, each word I spoke brought me that much closer to puking on her shoes.

I then turned and stared like a zombie at my laptop, which I had yet to turn on, pretending as if the last thirty seconds of my life had never happened. I would hide behind policy. If Betty didn't put in a helpdesk ticket, then I wasn't obligated to help her. I was simply being a good little worker bee.

Betty lingered for a moment, most likely unsure if I was going to add anything else, before huffing away like a child, complete with an exhaustive sigh that punctuated her frustration. It was a wasted gesture. I couldn't care less what she or anyone else thought of me.

Well, actually, that's not entirely true. I didn't *want* to care what others thought of me. I wasn't properly equipped for the harshness of reality like normal, non-depressed people were. Everyday downs felt more monumental than they should have, or how I thought they should feel, anyway.

My feelings now simply blurred together into a giant ball of fuck you, steamrolling me closer to oblivion with each passing day. I knew the people around me hated me—their hushed conversations were louder than they thought. Then again, maybe they meant them to be just loud enough to get their point across. But what they would never understand is that no matter how much *they* hated me, *I* hated myself an infinite amount more.

I rubbed my eyes—tired from the lack of sleep—and then reached across my cluttered and unhygienic desk. Pushing aside some stained papers and an open bag of chips that had been there for as long as I could remember, I grabbed my dark green coffee mug and turned it so the chipped part of the rim faced away from me. The pasty puke taste in my mouth reminded me that not all decisions were the right ones. And the last few beers that I had before passing out were definitely not a good decision. I needed to wash the taste away.

The mug was chilly and half full of Friday's coffee. I watched as the hardened island of cream floating in the center broke into tiny pieces as I swished it around, like a colony of ants fleeing their hill.

Just drink it.

I stared at the vortex I'd created in the

center of the mug, debating with myself before reluctantly taking a sip of the cold, lumpy liquid. Some caffeine was better than none, right? That was the idea. But the tactile nightmare that ensued quickly confirmed that I had chosen poorly, yet again. Some bits of the creamer dissolved on my tongue, while others kept their solidity well past their prime, forcing me to chew my mistake.

I reluctantly swallowed and put the mug back down.

I would have preferred fresh stuff, but I just couldn't bear the thought of going into the kitchen to get it. *The flock* congregated in there—the overly-happy, everything-is-great people in the office. They hovered around the coffee pot at random times during the day, constantly refueling their cheeriness with caffeine like it was all theirs to devour.

Another pointless conversation is what they would try to suck me into if I ventured too close. And rehashing my weekend with the flock, which consisted of undercooked TV dinners and at least one thirty-pack of Coors Light, was not something I needed at that moment. I didn't care how great their kids' lower case letters had become, or where they went for their latest family outing, or politics, or sports, or anything. I didn't give a crap about them because I didn't give a crap about me. Avoidance was now my best and only measure of defense, and I had become the damn master of it.

My shrink, Dr. Anders, told me that I needed to force myself into social situations if I was ever going to "hurdle over some of my problems." It was shortly after that when he started me on my meds. "Let the medication do its work," he said. "In about a month you should start feeling better." That was over a year ago. The pills had done little to stop the woeful spread of my depression. And, unfortunately, talking to him had done even less. But he tried, and that was more than most did.

If anything, the few good emotions I had left became so subdued it was as if they'd been tied-up, gagged, and stuck in a windowless room, never to be heard from again, eternal prisoners to my tyrannical depression. The sad thing is, I didn't know if I missed my feelings, having not felt them in so very long. What was it like to laugh at a movie? Or feel remorse? Or be genuinely happy about something, anything? Even sadness felt different, as if it had been saturated into something worse. But without my medication, I feared what I might become. More importantly, I feared what I might do.

Both of those fears were soon to be realized.

Someone cleared their throat behind me.

Slouched in my chair, I uncaringly looked over my shoulder, expecting to find someone else with a problem that I didn't care to solve.

"Phil," I said, sitting up instinctively. I didn't expect to see my boss so early in the morning. Then again, 11 A.M. probably wasn't early to those who still actually worked. I could count on one hand the times that Phil walked into my cubicle, and it was never just to say hi. And judging by the look on his face, this time was no different.

Phil's fifty-something-year-old genes grayed his hair, making him look distinguished and powerful. He was impeccably dressed in pleated black slacks and a finely-pressed, white button-down shirt. He was the antithesis of who I had become. Phil had pulled me into his office a few months back for what he referred to as a "chat." He told me he was worried about me—more specifically, my health. Apparently, my deteriorating work ethic fired off a flare that I refused to see while the rest of the office stood by, blinded by its failing glow.

"Can I see you for a minute, Sean?" Phil said, nodding towards his office on the far side of the floor.

My depression surged like the incoming tide. "Sure," I said. "Be right there." I rubbed my eyes as if doing so would remove the dark bags from beneath them. I then tried to fix my wiry head of greasy, unwashed hair with my hand, to no avail.

I sensed this was bad. Something in the air didn't feel right. My stomach knotted up. With depression came anxiety—waves of it actually — like an emotionally-driven tsunami. My crazy medication was supposed to handle both of them —the omnipotent pill if you will. It didn't help with either. At best, the meds helped to create an ultrathin membrane that held me back from the edge. And that membrane was about to burst.

The walk to Phil's office went by in slow motion. I followed him like I was being led to slaughter. My arms dangled by my sides. I dragged my feet along the worn, uninspiring, grayish carpet. Heads began to pop-up over the sparsely-decorated, pincushion cubicle walls one by one, like a community of prairie dogs on the alert. It was as if they sensed what was to come. Did they know something I didn't? Was there chum in the water that I now treaded? It was beginning to feel that way.

Phil stood beside his open door. A half-smile cut across his face in an awkward way. It was the kind of smile a person wore as more of a forced nicety in order to make the other person feel more comfortable. It just made me more nervous. My broken mind went into overdrive as it tried to figure out why I had been summoned, blindly ignoring the most obvious reason.

I dug my long fingernails into the skin on my thumb, picking until the rawness hurt and began to bleed. The pain helped me to stay in the now but poked at my headache at the same time.

I walked past Phil and into his office with my head down, like a scolded dog. He slowly closed the door behind me and drew the thin metal blinds that now hid us from the rest of the office.

"Please, sit," Phil said, motioning to the two red-padded chairs in front of his desk, each perfectly spaced from one another.

I sat with my hands folded on my lap and nervously looked around his immaculate office. I knew this wasn't good. That's why my foot tapped rapidly on the floor. I needed some way to expel the anxiety that clawed at my insides.

Every paper on Phil's desk was stacked neatly atop the other, almost as tidy as a fresh ream of paper. I recognized a few of the stacks as revenue reports for the company's *As Seen on TV* products that lined the pockets of the owners and made the rest of us enviously hate them.

Evenly spaced around the outer edge of Phil's desk was a kaleidoscope of family pictures: a gorgeous wife, Meghan, whose genes defied science by never aging; a handsome son and future Harvard attendee, Nick; a beautiful daughter, Emma, whose division-1 soccer team made State three years in a row; a nice house with an immaculately manicured landscape; and an adopted Greyhound named Dash. *Fucking Dash.* Phil had a perfect life. Or, what most people would envision as perfect, anyway. And while I admired what he had, I was enough of a realist to know it was something that would never be mine. The world had classes, and the classless need not apply.

Phil walked behind his desk and sat in his

chair.

"Listen, Phil, if this is about last week, I can explain." The words shot out of my mouth as if someone else was speaking them. I wasn't about to tell him that I just didn't feel like working and that's why I used a week of sick time. It was a week spent getting drunk, passing out, rinsing, and repeating. Another lost week of my life.

Luckily, for both our sakes, I wasn't given the chance to think of a lie on the spot.

"I'm sorry, Sean," Phil said. He breathed in deep and on the exhale said, "But we have to let you go."

I heard what he said. I just couldn't comprehend it at that point.

Phil continued. "Your work has really suffered over the past year, Sean. That can't come as a surprise?" He eyed me for a moment with his brow raised and his head cocked ever so slightly, as if waiting for me to agree.

No, it didn't come as a surprise. I knew I had become the poster child for slackers all over the world. I wasn't about to contribute to the conversation, though. Was I supposed to lambaste myself? Happily nod at the fact that I was all but worthless? Honestly, I had no idea how to feel. I had never been fired, but I could only assume I was supposed to be angry, or shocked, or something—anything. But only an unfeeling numbness coursed through me. So I just sat there with an empty look on my face.

Even if I had something to say, I didn't know if I could actually say it. My tongue felt heavy, as if it was suddenly coated in lead. My mouth was beyond parched. And my lips stuck together, as if they were glued shut, which was probably better for us both.

After an uncomfortable moment of silence, Phil continued. "Computers aren't built on time. Helpdesk tickets are stacking up. Some of them have been open for months now, Sean. And people are complaining about you. A few of those complaints have even been to HR." He paused and lowered his voice a bit, even though the office door was closed, and we were alone, and said, "Some of the complaints are pretty serious, Sean. Human Resources had no choice but to take things to the next level."

I assumed one of the complaints was from Martha Jenkins, that intolerable cow. How was I supposed to know she wasn't pregnant? She sure as hell looked it, with her bloated face and round belly. Not to mention the large flower-print moo-moo-esque tarps she had been wearing. Turns out she was going through a nasty divorce and leaned a little too heavily on food to cope. So when I chimed into a conversation—on one of my rare "good" days—and asked when the baby was due, well, she didn't take too kindly to my mistake. The conversation quickly became heated, and some choice words were exchanged, *fatty* being one of mine. I knew better than to get involved in one of their stupid conversations in the first place. It served me right.

Phil opened one of his drawers and removed some papers. "I've covered for you for as long as I could, Sean," he said. "Corporate told me I needed to make a change immediately. If I didn't, they would. I assumed you'd prefer to hear it from me."

I looked down at the floor as Phil spoke. I knew this was hard for him. I felt bad that he had to do it. Phil had always been good to me; better than he needed to be. He let me get away with more than any other boss would have. And at that moment, I felt guilty for putting him in the position I had.

Phil reached down for the small packet of papers he had removed from his drawer—four, maybe five pages worth—held together by a large black paperclip and embossed with Monutek's blue pyramidal corporate logo in the upper left corner.

"I was able to get you three month's severance." Phil handed the packet across the desk to me. "It's more than they usually give out. Trust me on that. But considering what you're going through--" He paused and looked away as if he shouldn't have acknowledged my mental *health.* My numbness made it impossible to care at that moment. After what he must have deemed to be an appropriate amount of time, he looked back. "I was able to get you a continuation of your health benefits for another six months. I tried to get you a year, Sean, but they wouldn't go for it. I'm sorry."

Not as sorry as I am.

I looked down at the packet. Wherewith and hereto were the majority of words. Legal jargon telling me that I'd been fired in the most convoluted of ways possible. I nodded while looking down at the papers, but not reading them. It was nothing more than a preventative measure to keep from crying. I wanted to curl up into a ball. My emotions had stampeded past the medicinal dam holding them back and crashed against my mind with an unforgiving force. Too many feelings, all of them bad, vied for my attention at once and overwhelmed me to the point where I almost shut down completely. It was impossible to know which feelings were there because of the situation and which ones just tagged along to burn me out quicker. Either way, they all sucked.

A few uncomfortable moments later, after I had listened to Phil apologize again for something that was clearly not his fault, he asked me if I had any questions. I shook my head. It was the best I could do. In reality, I had a ton of questions, but none that he could possibly answer. And none that I had the energy to ask.

I stood, though I don't remember wanting to stand, and moved for the door. I wanted out of that office as quickly as possible, to leave what happened right where it was. But like the clumsy idiot I had become, I opened Phil's door too quickly, causing the metal blind to smack loudly against it and garner the attention of what seemed like everyone on the floor.

Just go, I told myself. *Move your legs.*

I then took a deep breath and left Phil's office. What more was there to say?

The entire office stared at me like some kind of circus freak—a newly fired, sword-swallowing, bearded lady. *Step right up, folks.*

Come see Sean, the most hopelessly unredeemable person on the planet. Today only!

My stomach heaved as I pushed through my walk of shame. The lemmings would look at my face as they no doubt tried to piece together the story that no words could convey, then down to the termination packet in my hand, and then back to my face. A few smiles arched across the faces of those I shared a mutual dislike with. If anything, I was relieved to never see those heartless bastards again. But most of them had just tuned-in to the impromptu Monday morning fiasco that was Sean O'Rourke.

My head numbed further and made me almost too lightheaded to walk without holding onto the cubicle walls for support. My breath shortened and now came in silent gasps. After what felt like an eternity, I made it back to my cubicle and sat on my squeaky black chair for what would be the last time. I had to. Just for a second. I needed to collect myself from the oncoming panic attack. That, too, was something the medicine was supposed to help me with but never did.

Phil's sorrowful image reflected off my smudgy monitor as he stood behind me. He was making sure I wasn't going to do something stupid, like shut down the servers, or just go and delete everyone from the corporate directory. He had to. It's what a good manager did. And he was a good manager. But what Phil didn't realize is that I didn't care enough to do anything, let alone something stupid. I was long past the point of caring.

I stood, threw my jacket on as quickly as I could, and headed for the bank of elevators. I left my favorite mug and the rest of my meager personal belongings where they were; I wouldn't need them where I was going.

Phones rang, but no one answered them. People had stopped moving. They had stopped talking. An awkward silence weighted down the air, thick enough to feel like a heavy fog after a warm summer shower. I heard myself breathing as if my ears were stuck to my chest. *Am I hyperventilating*? I felt my heart pounding much faster than normal, like it would soon beat itself out into the open. *Am I having a heart attack*?

I thought my coworkers didn't care, but they did. They cared to watch my tragedy play out like some kind of stupid reality show. I couldn't blame them, really. I'd do the same thing. Misery was always at its best when you were a spectator.

I pushed the brushed-aluminum up arrow between the two elevators. The hazy images of my still-staring coworkers gleamed off the polished elevator doors like a gallery of semi-transparent ghosts. And just to make the moment that much worse, *my* disheveled reflection was more pronounced than the others. It silently mocked the disaster I had become.

My eyes appeared wet. *Am I crying*?

A subtle ding rang out, though it sounded more like a sonic boom in the enveloping silence. The elevator doors then thankfully slid open. I hurriedly walked into the empty car with my head down and my body numbed, as if I'd been shot with enough tranquilizer to take down a bull elephant. I then pushed the button for the twenty-fourth floor and kept my back to the office until the doors closed.

It only took a second for the elevator to begin its ascent and even less for me to start crying for real—bawl, actually. I tried to stop. It was no use. The tears streamed down my face like they had when I was a bullied child. My chest heaved uncontrollably. My lips quivered. My appearance and emotions were now one in the same.

The elevator ride was thankfully quick and uninterrupted. I didn't know how I would explain myself if the car had stopped. The "I've just got something in my eye" excuse didn't seem like it would fool anyone—not with my entire face glistening and my chest heaving like an asthmatic in the midst of allergy season. I didn't want to deal with people asking if I was alright. "No!" is what I'd scream back at the top of my lungs. "I'm not alright. I am as far from alright as one human could possibly ever be."

After a moment of pause, I stepped from the elevator—the weight shift jostling the car—and made my way across the narrow hall to the only door on the twenty-fourth floor. A sign that read "Do Not Enter - Alarm Will Sound" hung in the middle of its dented metal surface; its red letters were faded and peeling. I ignored the sign, as I had so many times before. The alarm was now nothing more than a grouping of frayed wires that slithered their way across an old brick wall and to the black outline of where the alarm panel was once affixed.

The cramped equipment-filled room was loud and packed with whirring and banging machines that gave life to the building below.

The extreme loudness was the very reason I liked it so much up there. My thoughts had to compete for attention, a competition they usually lost.

The twenty-fourth floor was my getaway back when I smoked cigarettes—something I gave up in hopes that it would improve my outlook on life. It was a stupid idea to quit. It was all those bad things the tobacco companies put in them, like arsenic, which made me think twice. My body was already brimming with poisons. I didn't want anything extra entering my system that could possibly lead me further astray. Turns out those short smoke breaks were something I needed more than I knew at the time.

I walked across the room and stopped when I reached the far wall. I knew myself well enough to stash a pack of Marlboro Reds for an occasion such as this. My predictably was sad. The fact that I knew that and couldn't change it was even sadder. I carelessly went to my knees on the dirty concrete floor and reached behind the large condenser unit as it clacked and banged. I palmed for the pack of cigarettes, thinking it might be gone after a few unsuccessful feels, but found it pushed back soon thereafter. With it came a white book of matches, attached by an elastic band and stamped with *Denny's Pub* across it.

There were many nights when I stumbled out of Denny's a few too many beers deep. And those were the nights I could remember; nights I hadn't blacked out on only to wake up the next morning in a pool of my own puke. Sometimes I was lucky enough to make it to my apartment building before that happened. And on the really good nights, I'd even make it all the way *into* my apartment.

I thought about ripping open the pack of cigarettes and smoking the whole thing in one giant puff, like a tobacco harmonica. That would be the rush I was looking for. But then it would be over. I couldn't have that. This singular joy needed to last as long as possible, like a death row inmate's last meal. I wanted to savor each cigarette, suck in every cancerous puff and relish in it for all it was worth.

I quickly tapped the pack against my hand, tore the cellophane off, pried open the top, and discarded the half-sheet of foil to the dusty floor. The first cigarette broke when I pried it free of the pack. I let it fall to the floor and then held out my hand. I hadn't realized they were shaking. I made a fist and tried to steady myself, but it didn't help. I knew nothing was going to at that point.

I closed my watery eyes and took a cleansing breath.

The next cigarette thankfully made it to my lips. Three matches later, it lit. I inhaled so deeply that I feared no air would be left for my next breath. The milky cloud flowed through the filter and felt amazing as it wafted into my lungs. The burst of nicotine sent a calming sensation shooting through my veins. I closed my eyes and savored the moment. If only every second of life could feel that good. That would be a life worth living for.

I looked to the cigarette as a tear dropped from my eye and wet its stem. "Why did I ever give you up?" I asked, with nothing but the machines listening. At least the cancer sticks didn't preconceive me to be the degenerate I actually was. I could still fool inanimate objects, for all that was worth.

I took another puff and savored it a bit too long. I then began to cough violently, followed by more uncontrollable weeping. I suddenly had no off switch. I hated myself on a level I never thought possible, a level I thought had been reached long ago, but one I had now come to find I had surpassed.

With my back to the old brick wall, I slid

down to the floor. I tucked my head between my knees and rocked gently, like a mental patient in a padded room. A steady stream of tears dripped from my eyes and dotted the floor beneath me. My emotions were stacked too high atop the other. This was something I'd known for a long time. And like a tower built on a crumbling foundation, I knew they would eventually collapse in upon me. I just hadn't prepared myself for when they did.

Being fired pushed me past the point where I still felt in control. I hated my job, but not for the work itself. I loved technology. And I used to enjoy doing what I did. It was the way I felt while doing it that had become too much: constantly having to fix other people's problems when I had no idea how to fix my own. My cluttered mind could no longer cope with it. It was a lot to handle for someone lacking the ability to do so.

I took another long haul from the butt, then another, and another until only the filter was left. I angrily flicked it across the room. Fresh air was what I needed. The room was suddenly much too cramped. The old brick walls felt as if they were closing in on me like quicksand. The machines judged me through their lifeless eyebolts and laughed through their arching welds.

Stop it!

I stood, lit another butt, and made my way up the metal ladder leading to the roof. The smoke stung my eyes as I held the cigarette between my lips. I climbed the seven quick rungs of the ladder and pushed on the rusted roof hatch. It didn't open. I pushed harder, knowing the ice storm the night before probably sealed it shut. It still didn't budge. I banged again and again. Anger, frustration, it all came out. I beat the door like I wanted to beat myself. The door finally creaked open, but I still banged, harder and harder, until my hand bled.

The pain hurt in a good kind of way. It drew my thoughts away from the situation, if even for only the briefest of moments.

I stopped banging but kept bleeding.

I then wiped my eyes, one at a time with my sleeves, and made my way through the open hatch. I'd gone over this day more than once in my head. The location changed each time, as did the method, but the result was always the same.

My hands were shaking more as I cleared the last rung of the ladder and climbed onto the icy roof. It could have been the frigid wind whipping through the gaps of the rooftop machines, or the cold drizzle that drifted down from above, still undecided if it wanted to be rain or snow. More likely it was my nerves. I zipped my coat closed and looked up at the grey winter sky, its color mirroring my own inner turmoil. I then took a step onto the ice and slid a ways until I hit a bare patch of wet, grainy tarpaper that stopped me short.

I used that opportunity to light another butt and take a long, satisfying haul.

The drizzle turned to rain as I moved more cautiously towards the edge of the roof. An anxious tingle tore through my body. I looked over the edge at the winter wonderland that I longed to be free of, down twenty-four stories and to the sidewalks that flowed with people. They appeared to be nothing more than tiny dots from my viewpoint. A city plow scrapped the slushy winter road with a line of traffic stuck behind it. Old, ice-coated buildings lined the street as far as I could see, somehow prismatic in their beauty, despite the bleakness they helped to create.

My mind raced. Thoughts zapped against the side of my head like bumper cars travelling at the speed of light.

Was this the right thing to do? I sure as hell

didn't know. I didn't care. My mind was made up.

Stop trying to talk me out of it!

Another few puffs and I flicked the cigarette over the edge. It drifted down on the wind and eventually vanished from my sight. I crushed the pack in my hand before I could light another and let it fall to the icy roof and slide off to the right—a few ground-up tobacco leaves spilled out and browned the slick ice. What was the use in smoking more? It didn't matter at that point. Nothing did. I could smoke all twenty butts and the only thing I'd be is colder, wetter, and less determined to see this through.

I inched closer to the edge. More adrenaline surged through me as a strong wind pushed against my back, willing me forward. It appeared at that moment that even the elements had grown tired of my existence.

I began to cry again.

The tears raced down my cheeks and leapt off my face over the edge of the building. I didn't try to stop them this time. I figured it was no use. We were going to the same place; they just had a head start.

I forced my watery eyes closed and took another deep breath of the cold air. My lungs burned, as if someone had jabbed an ice pick through the bottom of each of them, but pain was no longer a concern of mine. I had accepted the situation for what it was. I knew what I had to do.

My legs were shaking, wobbling as if they now lacked bones; I had to lock them up at the knee just so I wouldn't crumple to the ground. Something inside me begged me to stop, pleaded with me to reconsider. I ignored it. Why should I reconsider? This was my only way out. Something I had put off for too long. I was sick and tired of feeling this way.

I shivered, but not from the cold. I guess it was natural to be scared. I tried to think about my life, what I had, what I was about to give up. The sad thing was that I couldn't come up with anything of substance. Not one single thing.

In a way, it made what I was about to do easier.

I kicked off the ice crusting the roof's raised edge and cleared a place to stand. Without thinking, I stepped up slowly, using the nearby antenna to steady myself. While now ice-free, the edge was still slick from the seemingly unending precipitation.

My body tingled in fear as the front half of

my shoes slipped forward and hung freely off the edge of the twenty-four-story rooftop. My entire body was shaking, partly from the cold, the rest from nerves. I shut off my mind the best I could and tilted my head to the sky. I soaked in what I thought would be my final moments.

The sounds around me faded, as if someone had turned down the world's volume. The wind no longer howled, nor did I feel the chill of its bite. I was finally numb from the inside out and no longer susceptible to life's cruel grip.

Depression would not beat me. I wouldn't allow its stupid, maniacal hatred to control me a second longer. Not one single second. *You hear me*? I had accepted what was to be and should have been a long time ago. To take down an enemy, sometimes you had to scuttle the ship. And that's exactly what I planned to do.

In a final moment of self-pity, I closed my eyes, breathed in deeply, and leaned forward.

2

"I'd be careful if I were you," someone said from behind me. It was a man's voice, deep and confident.

I opened my eyes, startled to hear any voice at that point. I was still on the edge of the roof with only inches separating me from a freefall. But that wasn't right. I felt weightless, a victim to gravity only seconds ago. Yet there I was, dangling over the roof's edge, as if it had never happened.

Maybe I was more depressed than I knew. It wasn't out of the realm of possibility to think I was losing my mind altogether. Was I psychotic? Was I something worse? It was an extremely difficult few seconds for me. I wanted to look over my shoulder and see who the voice belonged to, but I was frozen in thought. Or maybe it was fear. I grasped at the wisps in my head, but failed to catch any.

Turn around.

Adrenaline still surged through me, pushing me to do something I could have sworn I already had. My heart tried to beat itself out of my chest with each pounding thump. My breaths came in short, sporadic gasps. Looking down at the street, I suddenly became scared. A moment ago, I was resolute in what needed to be done. Only seconds separated the two polar opposite thoughts. There was no way a sane person would be where I was at that moment, both mentally and physically. Not a chance.

On wobbly legs, I stepped back onto the roof from the icy ledge. I then turned to find a very tall man, maybe six-foot-four, staring at me with a look of concern emblazoned on his face, the obvious owner of the voice. He was dressed in a dark blue jumpsuit with the words *"Maintenance Department"* embroidered over his right breast pocket on a black patch with white lettering. He seemed out of place up there. But then again, anyone on the roof in the middle of winter would conceivably be out of place.

"I didn't know anyone else was up here," I said.

It was the first and only thing that came to mind. But why the hell was I still alive? I know I leaned off the edge. Burned into my short term memory was the cold air that violently stung the side of my face. But did I feel that? I patted my pockets for the pack of cigarettes to calm my nerves, realizing I had crushed the pack minutes ago. It was still crumpled into a ball and off to the side of the roof. I hadn't planned on needing them again.

Gravity seemed to push down on me a bit harder at that moment, further trapping me in place to wallow in my self-doubt.

The man in the dark blue jumpsuit smiled and looked up at the sky. "Will this cold and unforgiving winter ever end?" he asked, looking back at me.

His teeth were pristinely white and reassuring in a way. He then took a few steps closer to me, careful of the ice beneath his feet.

My mind raced with thoughts, none of them making any sense. One thing was clear though. I should be dead, splattered like a bug on a windshield. But instead, I found myself confronted by this janitor on a roof that I could have sworn I just leapt off. My heart throbbed inside my chest, to the point where I was sure I'd see my jacket pulsating if I looked down.

The man reached into his pocket. "Cigarette?" he asked, removing a pack of Marlboro Reds.

I stared at him after he said it. How did he know I wanted a cigarette? Then again, pretty much all smokers pat different parts of their bodies when looking for the rectangular pack. He must have seen me come up empty after my quick search. I didn't spend too much time wondering. I was too frazzled by everything that had happened in the last few minutes to concentrate.

I nodded and walked over. "Thanks." I took a butt from the pack and put it to my lips. My hands were surprisingly no longer shaking. Strange, considering how cold it was and how out-of-sorts I was. I patted my pockets, looking for the matches. No sooner had I started when the man handed over a black Zippo lighter with a knowing smile on his face.

"Thanks again," I said, flicking it to life. I inhaled and looked at the lighter, closing the hinged top as I did. I noticed the word *"Change"* engraved on its front. Because of the nicotine, my head felt lighter than the rest of my body, as if it was filled with helium. I quickly closed the lighter and attempted to hand it back.

"You keep them," the janitor said with a smile. "I don't smoke."

That seemed odd. But then he answered the question I hadn't asked.

"I found them today while I was cleaning," he said. "Someone left them in the bathroom." He then shook his head. "Lucky for them, I didn't catch them in the act. I don't tolerate those who break the rules."

"Oh," I said. I puffed on the butt. It was uncomfortable for me to just stand there smoking while he watched me, like a sad one-man show. I hadn't had a chance to come to grips with what had just happened. "What are you doing up here, anyway?" I asked, exhaling a thick cloud of smoke. While it was the last thing I actually wanted at that moment, small talk was all I could muster. The myriad of thoughts in my head popped like bubbles before I could see what they contained.

"I could ask you the same question," he said. He eyed me for a moment, almost as if he was studying me. He then nodded over his shoulder towards the roof hatch. "I saw you shimmy up that ladder. Nobody is supposed to be up here, you know." He punctuated his words with a serious stare. He then nodded to where I was just standing. "And what in the world are you thinking, standing on the ledge like that? You a daredevil or something? You very well could have fallen to your death."

I looked back over my shoulder. That was

the plan.

He studied me for another few seconds, as if I was some enigma that needed solving. "The name's Mack," he said.

I shook his outstretched hand. "Sean." Despite being out in the cold, his hands were remarkably warm. His grip fully engulfed my hand; his fingers were much longer than my own, almost touching the back of my wrist.

Another strong gust of wind blew across the roof and howled through any slit or crevice it could find. By the looks of the sky, another storm was coming in. A storm I should not have had to endure by all accounts.

"Well," Mack said after another minute of awkward silence, "You'd better finish up that cigarette and get back to work. I'm leaving for the day. Been here all night. And I'm not about to leave you up here by yourself to have an *accident*. No, sir. I don't need that on my conscience."

I laughed, but not because I found what he said to be funny. I had come to grips with the fact that I was officially loony bin crazy; had to be. There was no other explanation. I could no longer trust my own mind to even discern reality.

"What's so funny?" Mack asked, turning

towards the ladder.

"Nothing," I said, shaking my head slightly. I took another haul of the butt and then tossed it onto the roof, putting it out beneath my shoe. "It's just what you said about getting back to work. I don't have that problem anymore."

Mack seemed to soak in what I said, nodding very softly as he processed it.

Could he tell just by looking at me how much of a fuckup I was? How completely unimportant I was to the world around me? Hell, I didn't know. A crashing rush of depression hit me as I thought about it. If someone asked me what it felt like to be me, I'd have a hard time describing it. But the closest I could come, if I really gave it some thought, would be being buried one-hundred feet deep in a pit of perpetually hot tar for all of eternity. That would be a good start.

Mack looked down at his watch and then back at me. "Well then," he said. "Since you don't have anywhere to be, are you hungry? I was going to grab a bite to eat before heading home."

"Not really," I said. And I wasn't. Food was the last thing I wanted.

Mack again looked to his watch. "Well,

how about a drink then? It's happy hour somewhere."

He watched me struggle with the idea.

"I'm buying," Mack said, climbing down the ladder.

"I think I might just go home," I blurted out. "But thanks for the offer."

"Nonsense," Mack said. He waved for me to follow. He quickly disappeared from my sight down the ladder, not giving me a chance to say no again.

I looked back at the edge of the roof and then to the ladder. Those were my two clear choices. Either way I was going down. And I very well couldn't go jumping off the building now. I felt obligated not to kill myself in some convolutedly roundabout way. I didn't want to leave Mack with a lifetime of guilt for something he had no control over. My intent was never to hurt anyone but myself.

My moment of private suicide was gone for now. Gone, but not forgotten.

I looked to the building's edge one final time before following Mack down the hatch, closing it when I was clear. A bloody impression of my knuckles greeted me as the hatch door closed shut. I didn't bother with anymore small talk. I just followed Mack back through the busy machine room and to the elevators with my head down. It was a surreal moment, walking back through the room I had just left for what I thought was the last time.

Mack pressed the down arrow outside the elevators and rocked slightly on the heels of his brown cowboy boots. He hummed something familiar while we waited.

"What is that?" I asked. I knew that tune from somewhere.

He stopped humming and looked over at me. "Don't know the name of it." He scratched his shiny bald head and turned back to the elevator. "My grandmother used to hum it to me when I was, oh, around five years old or so. Helped get me to sleep on those nights I needed it. I guess it just stuck with me ever since."

It was so familiar, but I had no idea why at the time.

The ride down was thankfully quick and uninterrupted, just as the ride up had been. I followed Mack through the bustling lobby and out into the cold winter air. As the building's door swung shut behind me, I paused for a moment and looked up to the roof. My eyes then followed the trajectory I should have taken, all the way down to the street in front of me. That's where I should have landed, right there, in the middle of the cab-filled street. That sure would have gotten their attention on the fifth floor. But for whatever reason, there was the tiniest pang of relief buried somewhere deep inside of me that I hadn't jumped, piercing its way out from within the darkness draped over my soul.

"You know any good places around here?" Mack asked.

I looked up from the street. "I do." A liquid lunch was something I had made a habit of over the past year or so. I counted the minutes from the time I walked in late for work until an early lunchtime. If I could make it that far into the day, the rest would be a bit easier, albeit even more unproductive.

Mack smiled. "Lead on," he said, stepping to the side.

We walked down two blocks and then over one to Morrison Avenue. The sidewalks were half their width from the ever-growing piles of snow and the stampeding lunch crowds, so we didn't talk; we just trudged forward like the mindless cattle we all were.

I should ditch this guy.

It would be easy enough to lose Mack in the crowd. And it's not like I'd ever see him again, being that I'd just left Monutek for the last time. I had a lot of things going through my mind that I couldn't sort out. The most prevalent one was my failed suicide. How the hell was I going to make small talk over drinks with some janitor I didn't care to know?

None of those thoughts mattered as we arrived quicker than I anticipated, as if we had walked a hundred miles an hour.

I shifted from the sidewalk and into a small entrance off to my right.

"This place okay?" I asked outside of The Golden Mug, one of my frequent lunchtime watering holes. A large wooden sign carved in the shape of a frothy mug of beer hung above the door, creaking and swaying in the blustery wind. They opened at ten o'clock for the sad people, like me.

Mack looked up. "Perfect."

I was now unemployed, so free was my new favorite word. And with Mack offering to buy, I figured I might as well down a few and then make my next move, whatever that was. Decisions always seemed easier to make with a couple beers in me. Actually, I found that everything was easier after a few drinks. My inhibitions were strong, no doubt held down like a circus tent by the deep-rooted stakes of my depression. But a few beers always turned into a few too many, and my decision-making ability went downhill in a hurry.

I pulled open The Golden Mug's heavy wood door, which, for whatever reason, seemed lighter that day. A wall of warm air bit at my cold cheeks as the blood rushed back into them.

"Hey, Sean," the bartender called out, sadly reminding me we were on a first name basis. "The usual?"

I nodded. I was such a loser.

Aside from Tim, the bartender, the place was empty. Well, that is if you didn't count Richard. And I didn't. Eighty-five-years old, he was more like a part of the establishment than a patron. He was there before anyone and at times was the last to leave. He never said much, which was fine by me. He just sat at the end of the bar with his head down, sulking. Poor bastard seemed to dwell in a world I was all too familiar with.

Tim slid a Coors Light bottle in front of me.

I needed more than a beer, though. "I'll take a sidecar with it today," I said.

Tim eyed me, judging me silently, and then said, "What will it be?"

I looked behind the bar at the copious amounts of bottles mirrored in the glass behind them. I must have had something out of each of them over the years, but one always seemed to work better at erasing the day than the others.

"Tequila," I said. I figured I might as well make it count. "The cheap stuff, though. My buddy here is buying."

He shuffled over and poured the shot. He then put it in front of me and shifted down a stool to Mack. "And for you, bud?"

"I'll have the same, thanks," Mack said. He then pivoted in his stool and turned to me. "You said I didn't need to worry about you getting back to work earlier. Should I take that to mean you are in need of employment?"

"I guess you could say that."

Tim placed the shot in front of Mack and the bottle of beer to its left.

Mack wasted no time in bringing the shot glass up. "To unexpected moments," he said, clinking the shot glass down on mine before downing the tequila. His face shriveled. "The cheap stuff indeed." He then eyed the empty shot glass before placing it back down on the bar.

At times I wasn't even sure it was tequila.

Maybe Tim had a moonshine distillery set up in the back. Not that it mattered, really. It could have been dog piss for all I cared, as long as it worked the same drunken magic.

Mack chased the shot with a swig of beer. "So," he said, licking his lips. "Are you interested?"

I looked over at him. "In what?"

"A job."

"No offense, but I'm not really cut out to be a janitor."

And I especially didn't feel like cleaning up in a building I just got tossed out of. That was a level of awkwardness I'd never be ready to handle. My pride had dwindled over the years, but it was still there somewhere. Or at least I thought it was. Of course, like most things with me nowadays, that was open to interpretation.

"No offense taken," Mack said. "But I wasn't asking if you wanted to be a janitor." He smiled. "I push a broom because I enjoy the satisfaction it brings me. I like things tidy and organized. I don't need the pittance it pays me."

He must have been the only janitor in the world that enjoyed what he did.

I downed my shot and chugged my beer until the bottle was dry. I turned to Tim and gave him a nod. Another bottle slid down the bar, stopping when it reached my hand. I took a sip to stop the foam, then turned to Mack.

"So, if you're not offering me a job as a janitor, what are you offering me?"

"An opportunity to change things," he said.

I eyed him for a moment, waiting for him to break out in laughter and say "I'm just kidding," but he didn't. Instead, he continued to look at me placidly.

"You're serious?"

He nodded.

Less than an hour ago, I was fired. Then, I unsuccessfully tried to kill myself. Now, I was being interviewed by a janitor in a bar. Life followed a very strange path at times. I wasn't in the mood or the frame of mind to even be listening to him. But I had already come this far. And he was buying me drinks. I figured it couldn't hurt to see exactly what he was talking about. I'd need beer money until I decided what was to come next.

I said, "What do you mean change things?"

"So you're interested?"

"I didn't say that, Mack." I took another swig of my beer.

I had no idea what he was talking about. And I certainly didn't want to just jump into a job, being only an hour removed from my previous one. But a consuming sense of urgency overcame me. For whatever reason, I didn't want this "opportunity," as Mack put it, to pass me by. I didn't know why I had that urge. But at the same time, something pushed me to just get up and leave the bar without saying another word. Some things had changed, but my internal struggle still waged as strongly as ever, if not more fiercely.

Yet, despite being overly cryptic, Mack had me intrigued. "Okay," I said. "Tell me more."

Mack smiled. "The job may seem simple on the outside, but the work is actually quite complex. It requires patience and understanding. You need to finesse these situations into a resolution."

I wanted to stop him right there. Two things I lacked were patience and understanding. And I had never been one to master the art of finesse. But rather than speak up, I took another sip of my beer. I might as well let him finish before turning him down. It was as polite as I could get at the moment.

Mack continued. "In essence, you'd be fixing problems."

"Fixing what? Like, computer stuff?" I could only assume he knew I was a tech guy since he was a janitor at Monutek. It wasn't that farfetched.

Mack shook his head. "No, I'm afraid a reboot or a couple of mouse clicks won't help these issues." He took a sip of his beer and pulled in a bit closer to me, not enough to make me uneasy, but just enough to let me know what he was about to say was serious. "You'd be helping people like you do every day, except you would be assisting them in a different way than you're used to."

I looked over at him and laughed. This guy was clearly not as good at reading people as I had thought.

He wasn't done explaining. Either that, or the confusion plastered across my face told him to continue.

"Let me put it this way," he said. "Some people have problems that they can't solve for themselves. Problems with their lives in one way or another. That's where you come in."

"You've got the wrong guy for that," I said. He couldn't be asking me what I thought he was. He obviously had no idea who he was talking to. It seemed comical to the infinite degree. I couldn't fix my own damn problems. But just to clear up any confusion, I said, "So you're asking me to help people with problems in their lives? Is that right?"

Mack nodded.

"No thanks," I said, downing my beer. "I'm no counselor."

If only my shrink was there. He'd either be mortified at the thought of me helping others or die laughing on the spot.

Mack nodded softly and backed away a bit. He took a sip of his beer and redirected his attention to the LCD that hung on the wall behind the bar. Live news shots showed a building burning out of control, while some cheesy reporter with a spray tan gave his take on what had happened. No doubt he suspected foul play. It just made for better TV.

As I watched the news, something started to gnaw at my insides. I began to think about the very vague offer that was just presented to me. I don't know why, but I needed to find out more. The overwhelming compulsion to kill myself had subsided a slight bit. It was no longer an insatiable urge driven by the moment, but more of a lingering, ever-present feeling I couldn't shake.

I still wasn't sure if it was something I actually wanted to rid myself of. After all, it's not like it was a spur of the moment thing. It certainly wasn't the first time I considered offing myself. The reasons behind my willingness to kill myself were still there. But now that I had tried, and subsequently failed, the drive was somehow lessened. I didn't know how much longer I would be in this world. But until I figured all that out, I was going to need some form of employment to pay my way through.

I turned to Mack and said, "I think you'd be making a mistake hiring me for something like that."

"It wouldn't be me hiring you, Sean. I work for someone too. The same man you'd also be working for."

"So when do I meet him?"

"You don't." Mack was quick with his reply. "He'll communicate to you through me. That's just how it is."

Why I was even contemplating this was beyond me. The whole situation with the job, and the man behind the curtain, seemed beyond shady. However, Mack exuded a level of confidence that I found reassuring in a way. I couldn't quite put my finger on it. He felt familiar. I started to look at the man beneath the uniform and toss aside some of my preconceived janitorial notions. Mack was smooth, like a polished beach stone, without trying to be.

"Tim, another shot," I said. I was still too sober to make decisions.

"Make that two," Mack added.

Tim hesitantly poured two more shots and walked them down. He stopped in front of me with a look of genuine concern on his face.

"Slow down, Sean," Tim said. "Remember what happened last time."

I eyed him disdainfully. I remembered what happened quite well. I still felt the woman's hand smacking my face after my hand smacked her ass. It was an unusual impulse, but I had a full day of drinking under my belt, so I was a beer zombie by late day. She dropped me like a ton of bricks, and I quickly became the laughing stock of the entire bar. It was one of the main reasons I only went there for *lunch,* when it was usually empty, and no longer partook in my after work drinking activities there. Nowadays, I tended to drown my miseries in the privacy of my own apartment.

"What are you, my father Tim?" I said. I

don't know why I lashed out, but I did. And for whatever reason, I didn't feel badly about it either. I'd have to add heartless to the ever-growing list of terrible things I had become.

Tim shot me a disgusted look, the kind of look I'd seen more and more as the years went on. However, I knew he wasn't about to turn down business in the middle of the day, especially when old Richard was the only other person in there, and he was probably still sipping his first beer. Tim shook his head and walked to the other end of the bar. If he only knew how much of an insult it was that I just likened him to my father, he would surely kick me out for good. But if I wanted to drink myself stupid, I had every right to. I was a grown, unemployed, depressed man. What other reasons did I need to drink?

I turned to Mack. "Cheers," I said, downing the second shot. Sad thing was, it didn't burn going down. It might as well have been water.

"Cheers." Mack buried his shot too.

I took another swig of beer and then wiped my mouth with my sleeve. "So, is this like charity work or something?"

"You could think of it like that," Mack said. "It is for a good cause."

I never really thought of myself as the charity worker type. More often than not, it was me on the receiving end.

I said, "And this guy, your boss, what does he get out of it?"

Mack looked at me for a moment before answering. He then smiled. "Like me, he longs for that sense of satisfaction."

I stared at Mack for a moment, waiting for him to offer up more. He didn't. I felt like I should have dug deeper, asked more questions to Mack's cryptic replies, but I really didn't feel up to it. I was completely and utterly exhausted. I wasn't supposed to drink while on my meds. One of the many side effects was tiredness. I usually got around that by pounding a large energy drink before my binges, maybe mix in a Red bull and Vodka, or one of those energy shots. But this, whatever *this* was, was impromptu. I didn't have the proper amount of time to prepare.

I gave Mack's offer a few minutes of thought, which was more than I gave most things lately.

"I'm sorry," I said, "but I don't think I'm the right guy for the job." If I couldn't deal with just the thought of doing it, I knew I wouldn't be able to follow through when the time came to do the actual work. It was better for both of us this way.

I chugged the rest of my beer and put the bottle on the bar. "Thanks for the drinks."

"You're welcome, Sean." Mack reached into his pocket. "But one more thing before you leave." He removed a green glossy envelope and held it out to me. "Humor me and take this."

"What is it?"

"If you change your mind about the job offer, your instructions are inside this envelope. No pressure. This needs to be something you want to do."

I hesitated for a moment before taking the envelope and shoving it in my pocket. "Thanks again for the drinks."

"Anytime," he said with a nod and a smile. "I'll see you around, Sean."

And for some reason, I was sure he would.

3

I stepped from the sidewalk and up the small flight of stairs leading to my apartment complex. I pushed open the door with more force than it required, causing the industrial metal-and-glass beast to slam shut behind me, vibrating the entire entryway.

I eyed the wall of locked mailboxes to my right. I hadn't checked my mail in over a week, possibly two, and the small bronze box was probably bursting because of it. *Let it burst,* I thought. Ninety-nine percent of what I got in the mail nowadays was either junk or bills, neither of which I wanted to waste a single second of time opening. Just another thing I shouldn't be dealing with.

Over the years, I had become a social ninja, never to be seen or spoken to unless it was on my terms. It was a skill I had perfected. I took the stairs two at a time and avoided every squeaky floorboard on the way up as if they were colored in red florescent paint. Most of my neighbors were old and retired, always home, always on the prowl for someone to talk to. That someone would not be me. They led a lonely existence, but no worse than mine, so I never felt the guilt that some did to stop and talk to them. To me it was like nails on a chalkboard; an event to be missed at any and all costs.

I quickly arrived at the fourth floor and entered my three-room, hundred-year-old disaster that I called home.

The old radiator clinked over in the corner, giving off too little heat to make the room comfortable but just enough noise to agitate me to no end. Its newest coat of white paint came off in strips on the sides, like a banana peel, and collected in a small pile that I had no intention of cleaning up. I'd brought the heater's ironic lack of heat up to the landlord a few times. Each time, he'd come in and tell me how balmy it was in my apartment, sweating from every pore on his rotund, hair-covered body before leaving, having done nothing but bang his wrench against its casing a few times for good measure, causing the pile of paint chips to grow even more. He was my super, but he was far from living up to his title. But you got what you paid for in the city, and I paid the least amount that I could.

I threw my jacket on the couch to my right and headed directly for the fridge. I opened the door, grabbed the beer closest to the front, and quickly cracked it open. I didn't breathe until it was gone. Making sure I got every last drop, I crinkled the can's side. At that point, I needed its inebriating carbonation more than air. I threw the empty can in the sink and reached in for a second one, closing the refrigerator door in my wake.

With a fresh beer in my hand, I walked over towards my couch. It was then that my next door neighbor's blaring television shot out from the background and into the forefront of my thoughts.

"Harry," I said, banging on the wall separating me from my near-deaf neighbor.

Get your damn hearing aid fixed! I had grown tired of him lately.

Having done him a favor in the past that required me to go next door, I quickly realized why others in the apartment complex referred to him as Dirty Harry. If cleanliness was next to godliness, then I lived next to the devil.

"Harry," I banged again. I knew he couldn't hear me. He never could. But it helped to release some anger, something I seemed to have a lot of lately.

I walked over to my favorite black leather chair and fell back, exhausted. What a rollercoaster of a day it had been already. I then picked up the cable remote and flicked on my TV. I turned up the volume past my comfort level, enough to drown out Harry's.

Hours passed. I'd down two or three beers and then piss like the well-oiled drinking factory I had become.

I looked over at the digital clock on the microwave. That's when the realization hit me that I was stone cold drunk. No matter how hard I concentrated on the green digital numbers, they continued to float around in circles and blur together.

11:45? Or was that 1:45 in the morning? Either way, it didn't feel good.

I stood from my chair and swayed in place for a minute, trying to steady myself. The spins hit me hard and fast. The walls of my apartment spun faster and faster, as if I was being sucked down a vortex, like Alice down the rabbit hole. I closed my eyes, but the world kept spinning. Once it started, it was already too late. My stomach lurched. I tried to bring my hand to my mouth, but it did little. A goopy combination of beer and bile came shooting out of my mouth and nose, covering everything within a foot of me, trickling through my fingers and down my arms.

My first impulse was to laugh. Laugh at my misery, at how sad I'd become.

My throat burned.

I dropped to my knees and hovered over the pile of puke, swaying slightly, and heaved some more. The rank puddle below me sloshed and splattered. I stared at the puddle, praying I wasn't about to go face first into it. When no more beer was available to throw up, bile solely took its place. When the bile was gone, I dry heaved.

I felt like I was going to die.

I wanted to die, still, again.

When my stomach had had enough, I wiped my mouth with my sleeve and stumbled over to my bed. When my head hit the pillow, the blackness took over.

4

Sunlight beamed through the numerous holes in my shades, making my monumentally painful headache pound that much harder. Crusty patches of puke caked my face and hair and left yellowing bile stains on my pillow. Sadly, it wasn't the first time I had woken up in that condition. Even sadder, the last time this happened was yesterday.

I looked over at my clock. 1:36 P.M. The numbers were no longer floating in circles, but their dim light was enough to add to my headache. I'd apparently slept through the entire morning and into the early afternoon. I contemplated just going back to sleep. Lord knows my head would have appreciated that. But instead, I found myself eager to brush my teeth and free my mouth of the rancid taste of last night's binge. I slowly shifted upright and put my feet on the cold hardwood floor.

My first instinct was to throw up. Thankfully, my stomach had nothing left to give.

It was as if someone repeatedly beat the side of my head with a rubber mallet. My entire face felt like it was going to explode through my eyes and let what little was left of my damaged brain ooze out the sockets.

I made my way over to the bathroom, past the pile of regurgitated beer that overtook all other scents in my shithole of an apartment. *I'll clean that up later*, I thought. But would I? Probably not. All I knew is that I didn't have the willpower to do it then.

A few pounding steps later and I made it to the bathroom. I flipped on the light, but my headache forced me to reconsider. I then opened the medicine cabinet and grabbed the bottle of Excedrin Migraine. I shook out three of the white pills into my hand, quickly deciding to make it four, and popped them into my mouth. I turned on the faucet and drank a gulp of water, swallowing the uncoated pills with it.

I then lumbered back to my bed and sat down, staring at the far wall and hating every second of my existence. This was no way to live. I was an embarrassment to the human race at that point. I'd known that for a long time, so it's not like I was fooling myself into believing something that wasn't. My life, what it had transformed into, anyway, was something best dealt with drunk. My problems were quickly shoved aside by the booze. I liked that place better. The next morning though, or afternoon as it were in this case, is when reality knocked on my door and refused to go away until I answered. Unemployed, hung over, and nearly broke was my new reality. And it wanted some attention in the worst possible way.

With my hand to my forehead, I tried to rub away the pain to no avail. I then leaned back against my headboard and slid down to my crusty pillow. I flipped it over to discover the same on the other side. It was then that I felt something sharp rub against my leg from inside my pocket. I reached in. The shiny green envelope was still there, its corner digging into my skin. It was folded, just like when Mack had given it to me. I'd forgotten about it entirely until that point. In fact, I'd forgotten about Mack.

I sat up and removed the envelope. I unfolded it and flipped it over, blank on both sides. With the care of a six-year-old opening a Christmas present, I tore the top off and looked in to find a single piece of folded off-white paper. When I unfolded the paper, ten crisp one-hundred dollar bills fell out and fluttered down onto my bed like browning leaves caught in a gust of wind. I certainly wasn't expecting that. I pushed the money aside and stared at the piece of paper in my hands, wondering if it was all some cruel joke. The paper had no job offer on it, nor did it have a job description, hours, anything like that, not even a name. The only thing written was my address in blue ink. Or, to be more precise, my building's address with apartment 810 scratched beneath that.

What the hell does this mean?

I stared at the piece of paper for thirty or so minutes, dazing in and out of reality, and dealing with my headache and the feeling of nausea it brought with it. Despite my current physical and emotional state, something drew me to find out who was in apartment 810. I ached from the inside out, but it was almost as if the paper in my hand was talking to me, guiding me in a direction I didn't feel like going.

Was it coincidence that Mack gave me an address upstairs? Or was this all planned in some kind of twisted way? There was only one way I was going to get the answer, but curiosity wasn't enough to drive me to find it. I felt too close to actual shit to care at that moment.

Just as I closed my eyes again, the phone started ringing, ring after annoying ring, until the answering machine finally picked up.

"Mr. O'Rourke, this is Harold Smith," the man said. It wasn't the first message from him. He worked for the people that owned my apartment building. I was a few months behind on my rent, but they acted as if I owed them a year's worth. "Consider this your official notice," he said. "You have thirty days from today to pay your back rent as well as three months forward, or you will be evicted. Have a nice day." He hung up.

Fuck you.

Just when I thought my life couldn't get any worse, it inevitably always did.

I scratched my scraggly beard and then looked at the address in my hand again. I then eyed the one-thousand bucks on my bed. It sure would solve some problems, my rent being one of them. Curiosity aside, I knew I now had to go up to apartment 810. Either that or try and kill myself again. But I was too hung over for that just yet.

5

After taking an excessively long shower, in which I fell asleep standing up at one point, I picked through one of the many piles of dirty clothes on the floor. I searched for the cleanest garments that I could find, something not stained with puke or some mystery liquid. It was surprisingly more difficult than it should have been.

Rummaging through my clothes reminded me of when I was a child, stricken with pneumonia and stuck at home for two weeks. I threw up for three days straight. I couldn't even keep down a glass of water, and anything I could keep down eventually ended up on my clothes, as I continuously missed the small plastic basin my mother had set next to me. When my fever hit 105 degrees, my mother took me to the hospital. They stuck me on an IV and filled me up with antibiotics. A few days later, my fever broke and they sent me home. But I never forgot the pile of clothes in my bedroom, stained and smelly, a reminder of what I'd just gone through.

This current pile of filthy clothes was now

a hyperbole for what my life had become.

I finally came across some ragged blue jeans and an old grey Abercrombie sweatshirt, neither of them stained. At least not that I could see. They would do. I figured I might as well be comfortable, albeit a bit malodorous, considering I had no idea what I had in store for me upstairs.

I grabbed my keys but paused before opening my door. It seemed like the next logical step: to go upstairs and see what the deal was with apartment 810. But was it a step I was willing to take? My usual feelings of inhibition held me back, tugged at me to stay put. What did I hope to accomplish by going up there anyway?

A thousand bucks in your pocket. That's what.

I opened my door without giving it anymore thought and left my apartment driven by a combination of curiosity and a need to pay my rent.

Deftly using my social avoidance skills, I took the stairs two at a time, as was the norm, and quickly arrived on the eighth floor, out of breath and now more nauseous than I was before. I walked down the hallway until arriving at apartment 810. The zero on the door's numbers had lost a nail and hung precariously upside down.

I stood in front of the door like a statue, unsure of what to do next. It was quiet enough up there that I could hear a very faint but distinct sound coming from the other side of the door. It sounded like someone was crying. I should know. I frequented that emotion quite a bit lately. But the fact that someone was crying made me weigh my options then and there. I hadn't committed yet. Nobody knew I was standing there. Mack didn't know that I had opened the envelope. I could run back downstairs and hide in my desolate cave of an apartment. Who was I to purposefully intervene on someone else's sadness? More importantly, what in the world did I hope to accomplish?

On the other hand, I could knock. And that's just what I did.

Why did I just do that?

I had committed to the feeling of spontaneity, something I knew nothing about. Some part of me didn't want the knocks to be heard as they weren't forceful at all, closer to taps, really. But they seemed to be just strong enough, as the sobbing stopped. I stood there and listened, unintentionally holding my breath, as if whoever was inside could hear me breathing. It must have been at least a couple of minutes before the crying started again, this time a bit louder and more emotionally charged.

The same part of me that made me knock like a newborn baby was now trying to talk me out of it completely, make me run away and hide from my own fears. Avoiding social interaction as I did made it more difficult to be social when forced into it. I was rusty to say the least.

I knocked again, this time with conviction. Maybe too much force, really. I felt like I should've shouted, "Police. Open up."

The crying again stopped.

"Who is it?" asked a woman from the other side of the door a moment later.

"Ah…" What was I supposed to say? "My name's Sean. I live downstairs on the fourth floor."

You couldn't think of anything better?

I looked around the hall uncomfortably, waiting for a response that didn't seem to be coming. What the hell was I doing up there? I still had time to run.

I turned back towards the stairs when the door opened a bit, not enough to be inviting, but just enough to see the chain lock still firmly attached. A woman, I'd say in her early thirties, peered out from within.

"Can I help you?" she asked. Her face glistened with tears.

"Well," I said, "I don't really know what to say to that." She looked at me like I was crazy. I felt crazy. *You are crazy*. "The thing is, I think I'm here to help you, actually." I really should have gone over this beforehand.

She closed the door suddenly, but softly. She then unlocked the chain and reopened it.

"I'm sorry," she said as she gently wiped her eyes with a tissue. "Do I know you?"

"No, I don't think we've met. It's just, I heard you crying and I wanted to make sure everything was alright."

Her curly blonde hair came down past her shoulders, partially obstructing her face. She gracefully swept it behind her ears and smiled the sweetest of smiles despite her apparent pain. Her eyes were red and swollen, but not so much that the bright blue couldn't pierce through like drops from the purest ocean. They were beautiful. She was beautiful. Strangely enough, despite her radiance, I wasn't attracted to her, not physically anyway. Maybe that was an effect of the meds, too.

"That's awfully nice of you to be worried

about me like that," she said, sniffling. "But I'll be fine." She looked at me and fought back more tears.

Whatever was affecting her seemed to be bone deep. She thought she was hiding it, but the pain seeped into the open as if she was sweating it out. I was a pro at detecting mental anguish, usually my own.

What to do now was the question? I didn't want to pry into this woman's life. But for whatever reason, Mack had sent me there to help her. He paid me to help her. And the money felt good in my pocket. But maybe I was placing too much trust in a person I had a couple drinks with. A wave of anxiety suddenly shot through me. I was just some weirdo knocking on stranger's doors, nothing more than that. This wasn't like me. I wasn't accustomed to spontaneously running off and doing the unexpected. *Oh God, what am I doing?* I really should have thought it out more. *Here comes the panic attack.*

"You said your name is Sean?" she asked, again wiping the tears from her eyes.

I nodded. I shouldn't have told her my name. *Was I breathing funny?*

"Isabella," she said, putting her hand to her chest.

"I'm sorry to bother you, Isabella." I knew I should say something else, but I couldn't find the words. So I stood there looking stupid. At least I was getting good at that.

We stood there looking at each other. It couldn't have been more than a few seconds, even though it felt like years. I could tell by her furrowed brow that she was wrestling with a thought. The thought a person weighed out for the positives and negatives before making the kind of decision made too quickly to really know if it was the right one.

"This might sound strange, but-" she said, stopping short. She wrestled with the thought a bit more before giving in. "Would you like to come in for a cup of coffee, Sean?"

As soon as she said it, I could tell she regretted it. I'd give her an easy out. "No, that's okay," I said. "I wouldn't want to inconvenience you." I knew I should take the opportunity to find out why I was up there, but I found myself conscious of her feelings, which in itself was strange as I hadn't thought about anyone else's feelings in a very long time.

She thought about it, but answered me quickly. "It's no inconvenience, really." Her demeanor had changed slightly. "It would be nice to have company right now." She still had apprehension in her eyes, but I think she realized I wasn't some deranged serial killer. But then again, the best serial killers were always the ones who blended in and never drew attention to themselves. Hopefully, the same depressing thoughts didn't run through her mind.

"Okay," I said, following her into her apartment. "I'd love a cup of coffee." I was acting instinctively. There wasn't any sort of logic to go along with what I was doing. I didn't want coffee. I wanted to go back to bed, as even talking the little I did made my head pound more.

She turned around as I stepped over the door's threshold, stopping me short. "This goes against my better judgment, you know."

"What does?"

"This whole "inviting a stranger in for coffee" thing. It's not something I typically do."

I smiled. "Don't worry. I'm about as harmless as they come." Didn't smell very good and looked like a vagabond, but I was harmless. That much was true.

She eyed me for a moment. "I know. I get a good vibe from you." She then turned and continued down the hallway. As she was walking, she turned over her shoulder and said, "Plus, since you live downstairs, you know how thin these walls are. And I can scream like a banshee." She smiled.

I thought of Dirty Harry and his blaring television as I followed her into her living room.

She said, "So, you could really hear me crying from the hallway?"

"It wasn't that loud, really. Just caught my ear is all."

Her living room was laid out the same as mine, except much cleaner and thoroughly organized. It smelled better too, like roses or some other kind of overly-fragrant flower. Whatever it was, it was a far better scent than that of stale, regurgitated beer. While the setup of our apartments was similar, her view was far superior to mine. I had an alley, frequented by some of the more unsavory characters in the city, while Isabella had an unobstructed view of the park across the street. While it wasn't much to look at now during the winter, it prettied up nicely in the summer.

"Sorry it's so hot in here," she said, nodding towards the same clunker of a heater I had in my apartment. "The super says it's working perfectly." She shook her head. "Even though he can barely make it out of here without sweating himself into a puddle."

"Funny," I said. "Yours is too hot and mine is too cold."

She laughed. "We just need to find baby bear's heater."

I looked back, unsure of what she was talking about.

"You know, Goldilocks and the Three Bears?" She waited. "My porridge is too hot, mine is too cold, mine is just right?" She looked at me as if I had two heads. "Didn't your Mother ever read that to you when you were a child?"

She might have read it to me. The bad parts of my childhood seemed to overtake the good parts, though. Either way, I knew the nursery rhyme. My wit just moved at a snail's pace compared to Isabella's.

I smiled. "Ah, I get it."

She sat on the couch against the wall. "Please, sit," she said, nodding towards a chair across from her.

I sat in the faded yellow chair; its flower pattern was barely noticeable, worn from time. I sank deep into the comfortable cushion as it enveloped me on both sides. I wanted to speak, but I couldn't find the words. My head still pounded from the night before. And now that I thought of it, I forgot to take my crazy pills. Maybe that explained some of my anxiety, but I doubted it. I knew the pills did little to help, but psychologically I felt more depressed and anxious knowing that the medicine wasn't inside me.

"You said you were here to help me?" Isabella said.

I saw the confusion in her eyes. Confusion we shared. "I did say that, didn't I?"

She nodded, smiled.

"Here's the thing-" The thought finished in my head before I could speak it, making me realize how stupid it sounded. But I had already started so I couldn't just leave it hanging. Plus, what else was I going to say? The truth and any lie I could come up with would share the same amount of absurdity. "I got this yesterday." I handed her the piece of paper with her address on it. I figured that complete disclosure would help.

She looked it over, her brow furrowed, and then quickly handed it back. She had a bruise on her forearm, about the size of a silver dollar, still more yellow than black and blue. A new one. I didn't think anything of it at the time.

"Okay, so you have my address," she said.

"There's more to it. Do you know a tall man by the name of Mack? Has a real deep voice?"

She thought for a second. "I don't think so."

I took the paper back and stuffed it in my pocket. Of course she didn't know Mack. Why would she? Nothing seemed to explain why I was there.

"So," she said, "this guy Mack gave you my address?"

I nodded.

"And he told you what? That you were supposed to come see me?"

"No, he actually didn't tell me anything."

As she started asking me questions, I realized that I should have reasoned all this out with myself before taking a step up the stairs to the eighth floor. Now this entire situation sounded as insane as I was.

"He offered me a job," I said. "He said the job was to fix problems. People problems." I shook my head. I couldn't believe the words were actually coming out of my mouth. "I told him I wasn't interested, but he gave me an envelope and told me my instructions were inside if I changed my mind."

"So I take it you changed your mind?"

"I guess I did."

"And my address was inside that envelope?"

I nodded.

"I see," she said, sitting back on the couch.

She appeared uneasy with that information. I know I would be if some strange man handed me a piece of paper with my address on it. It screamed stalker, or worse. I was uncomfortable because I felt like I was making her uncomfortable. The whole situation was just ridiculous. Now I'd be known as the creepy guy downstairs. She'll tell her neighbors and then word would spread and people would whisper about me as I walk by, more so than they already did.

Get up and leave. You've done enough damage.

"You nervous?" she asked, nodding down at my feet.

I hadn't even noticed. My right foot drummed on the hardwood floor, tapping out my emotions with each annoying click of my heel like it had in Phil's office yesterday.

"Sorry," I said. "I just feel like an idiot right now. I have no idea why I came up here."

"To fix my problems, right?" she said with a smile. She stood from the couch and made her way into the kitchen. "How about that cup of coffee?"

"Sure," was my reply.

I really wanted a beer. Not because that's what would satisfy my thirst, because at times it seemed unquenchable, but because it would help with my hangover in a beat-me-while-I'm-down sort of way. I wasn't about to go asking for liquor though. I sensed whatever was going on right now was built upon a cracked eggshell. Isabella was being overly nice to me, considering the circumstances. And I didn't want to overextend her hospitality. Plus, I knew that one beer would last me a minute at most, and that's if I purposefully sipped it. After it was gone, I would surely want another. That's not the kind of first impression I wanted to make. But looking down at my wrinkled clothes, I realized that impression had already been made.

While she fixed us the coffee, I stood up, walked over to the windows, and gazed out.

"You have a much better view than me," I said. It was a partially sunny day, but I knew the sunshine painted a better picture when looking from the inside out. It was probably below zero again.

"You must be on the south side of the

building?" she said from the kitchen.

"Apartment 439."

"So you must know Mrs. Johnson? I think she's right down the hall from you."

I knew her alright. The last time we spoke, I was drunk as a skunk. Turns out, she was a recovering alcoholic and a born-again Christian. A great combination to avoid. So when she came down the hall preaching the good word on sobriety and how the lord healed her, I told her in more or less words that she was a sour old bitch. Actually, no, I'm pretty sure that's exactly what I said to her. I then tried to force the bottle of vodka I had on me into her hands. "Drink," I told her. "Be merry for a change." She stormed away and slammed the door to her apartment. Having conjured up that memory, I thought it best to remain silent to Isabella's question.

"How do you take your coffee?" Isabella asked, poking her head out of the kitchen.

"Cream, if you have it."

"Milk okay?"

"Yes. Thanks." *Or if you don't have milk, some Bailey's will do.* I brought my hand up and pinched the bridge of my nose. *Damn headache. Go away.*

"Here you go," she said, stealthily moving

back into the living room a moment later. She put down a mug of coffee on the glass table separating us.

She then took a brown elastic hair tie from around her wrist and pulled her hair back into a loose ponytail. She had great bone structure and a defined jaw line and cheeks. Overall, a nicely proportioned face. With her hair now pulled back, another bruise came into view, this one on her neck. It looked older than the one on her wrist, more black and blue than yellow. The bruises could have been from anything. Her arms were toned, not much fat on her that I could see. She looked like she worked out, so it could have been from the gym. Not that I would know, having never been to a gym. But that was my best guess.

"How long have you lived here?" she asked, taking a sip of coffee from the mug she cupped between her hands.

"A little over five years." It seemed like an eternity though.

Isabella cocked her head a bit. "Five years? Really? I can't believe we've never crossed paths."

"I don't come out much." For all I knew, I could have passed her a million times in the hall. My head was always down in my perpetual sulk.

"Do you work around here?" she asked.

I opened my mouth to answer, but nothing came out. Up until then, the thought had been pushed from my mind. But there it was again, front and center, the spotlight on it.

"I *did* work at Monutek, down on Sidney Street."

She looked at me, no doubt wondering if I meant to say it in the past tense.

"I was laid off yesterday."

"I'm so sorry," she said. "I didn't mean..."

"No need to be sorry." I took another sip of coffee. The hot mug felt good in my hands. My circulation wasn't all that great, so my hands were always cold. "I needed a change of pace, anyway." I forced a smile. It sounded good, but it wasn't reality. I did need a change, but a change on my terms, and using my timing. But that was life, a big wet slap to the face.

The picture-filled mantel behind Isabella caught my eye. She was in a majority of them, some big, some small, a few collages. Each picture of her radiated happiness.

She must have noticed me staring behind her because she looked back over her shoulder. She soon turned back and smiled. "They remind me of the good times in my life.

Without family and friends you have nothing, right?"

I nodded slowly and kept looking at the pictures. I guess that meant I had nothing.

Most of the pictures seemed to be from her past, nothing too recent that I could see. Did that mean she wasn't happy now since her *good times* were in the past? Maybe I was reading too much into it. There was one picture laying face down at the end of the mantel.

"I think one fell down," I said, nodding towards it.

She didn't look. She didn't answer. Her smile faded a bit.

I should have kept my mouth shut. Now I was the one who was prying. But how could I help if I didn't ask questions? Then again, was I supposed to ask questions? It was so frustrating, like putting together a one-thousand-piece model ship without any sort of directions, or for that matter, glue.

We sat in silence and sipped our coffee. It wasn't as uncomfortable as it was before, with the proverbial ice having been broken, but I still didn't know what to say. I tried to come up with stuff to talk about, and from the look on her face, so did she. By all accounts, I was forcing this woman to have coffee with me. She didn't look like she needed all that much help. Yes, she was crying, but that could have been about anything. Hell, I cried all the time. I certainly didn't know her well enough, if at all really, to come out and just ask her what was troubling her. Like I had told Mack, I was no counselor.

I was thinking too much. So much so, that a bit of paranoia set in. My heart began beating faster, even though I was still sitting. Sweat seeped through the pores in my forehead, parking beads Isabella undoubtedly saw. The situation began to escape my already loose grasp. I couldn't even carry on a civil conversation any more.

"Thanks for the coffee," I said, placing the almost-empty mug down on the coaster on the table. "I better get going." I stood from the chair. I felt a panic attack coming.

"Oh, okay." She looked surprised by my sudden decision to leave.

I was just as surprised as she was. But this felt like the moment to go. I smiled and started to walk down the hall towards the door.

"I'm glad we met," I said, turning around. And I truly meant that. I hadn't really taken pleasure in meeting anyone in a very long time. It felt foreign, but in a good way. It was nice to know that I wasn't the only one with problems in the world, in some kind of strange, selfish way.

"It was nice to meet you too, Sean."

"I'm sorry I couldn't help with your problems," I said, opening the door. "I guess I had the wrong address."

She smiled. "But you did help. I'm not crying anymore, right?"

I thought about it and nodded softly. I guess some help was better than none. But did I give her the help that Mack had intended? Had I done my job? I doubt it, at least not one-thousand dollars' worth of work. Even thinking about that made my head pound more. I think the caffeine from the coffee made it beat to a louder drum.

The hall was as empty as it was when I arrived, still quiet except for the pleasant absence of Isabella crying. I wondered if she had to deal with the same type of old lurkers that I had to on the fourth floor. She was personable though, unlike me. She most likely didn't avoid human interaction at all costs.

I turned back, "See you around?"

She smiled. "I hope so."

And for the first time in a long time, I hoped so too.

6

I don't know why, but I felt emotionally lighter after leaving Isabella's apartment. My head was still dominated by the darkness. And I was still grossly hung-over. But it was almost as if an unexpected pinprick of light punched through the darkness and screamed from a million light years away to be noticed. I hadn't done anything to help her. Nothing concrete, anyway. But I wasn't about to dismiss my own feelings because of it. It felt good to feel good. At least for a few seconds. But despite me realizing that, something inside me tugged at that feeling, trying to dismiss it outright.

I walked down a few flights of stairs, going over what had just happened, trying to gain some insight into what I was doing, when the lights overhead began to flicker. I stopped on the landing of the fifth floor and watched as the stairway blinked in and out of light. It wouldn't be the first power outage in the older building. But I wouldn't put it past the cheap bastards I had for landlords to have not paid their bills.

Then the lights went out completely, aside from the single bulb directly above me. With no windows in the stairwells, it was next to impossible to see anything.

The air felt soupy and thick. My first thought was that the air conditioning went off with the power. But it was winter. The air conditioning wasn't on half the time in the summer. That couldn't have been it. And when I stopped to listen, I realized that all of the ambient noises, of which the building had many, seemed to vanish.

Something didn't feel right. A huge wave of depression slammed into me like a freight train, weakening my knees. My throat became tight and dry. It was difficult to find any saliva. I tried to fight it, to think about Isabella and that pinprick of light, but my thoughts were shoved aside. My depression felt like it couldn't be stopped at that moment, surging at a million miles per hour, straight for me.

These panic attacks hit really hard at times, and without warning.

"Hello," I said, both to see if I could hear it, which I could, and because I had a strange feeling I was no longer alone.

I peered over the railing towards my floor. It was as dark as dark could be, as if the landing I stood on had been swept away into a black void. I then looked back up to the floor I just walked down from. It was also pitch black. The only light still on was the one right above me, a single, dangling, flickering yellowish bulb. It was so silent that I could swear I heard the filaments burning away in the bulb.

"Is anyone there?" I called out again. There was no echo.

And then the single bulb above me went out, casting me into complete darkness.

"Hello?" I said again, almost in a whisper. At that point, I didn't want to hear anyone answer me.

What the hell is going on?

A shadow bolted from my right. Another from my left. I blinked. I knew my eyes hadn't adjusted to the darkness yet. That's all it was, right? At least that's all I hoped it was. But what if it wasn't? How were there shadows without any light? I really wasn't well. The panic attack was crippling now. Hard to breath.

Then I heard wheezy, forced breathing from somewhere in front of me. Somewhere much too close. And from someone that wasn't me. The sound sent a powerful chill up my spine. I held my breath to listen.

The light above me blinked back to life. When it did, I jumped back and hit the wall behind me.

What the fuck?

My heart raced.

"Hello, Sean."

A short, skinny man, emaciated to the bone, stood at the top step of the staircase leading down. He had long and scraggly jet-black hair, patchy and sparse. His face was ghostly white with dark circles below his eyes. I wish it had been miles, but no more than a few feet separated us.

"Who are you?" I said, with my back still firmly against the wall. I didn't like being there, not one bit.

The man ignored my question. "The bald man isn't who he claims to be." His voice was raspy. His teeth were yellow and stained, some of them missing entirely. "You would be best served to forget you ever met him."

I wanted out of there, to run as fast as I could, but I felt stuck to the floor, as if I had been cured into a new patch of concrete. I was quite literally frozen in fear.

"M-Mack?" I stuttered, still trying to figure a way out of this. "Are you talking about Mack?"

The sickly-looking man's eyes widened but he refused to answer. He seemed dangerous in a pitifully deranged sort of way.

"What do you want?" I asked.

The man crept closer to me. His right leg was stiff, not bending at the knee. He smelled like the soupy liquid that gathered at the bottom of a trash can, rancid and unwanted. He only came up to my chin, but I feared him as if he was a hundred feet tall.

"If you know what's good for you, you'll stop helping him before you start," the skinny man said, his breath rank. "I'll be watching you, Sean. I'll be watching you very closely." He flashed his gapped smile again.

The single bulb above me went dark again.

I didn't waste a second. I bolted up the stairs, feeling for the railing as I did. I wanted to go down, but that's where he came from. And anywhere at that moment was better than the fifth floor landing. I climbed until I was out of breath. I had no idea what floor I was on, but there weren't enough floors in the building to separate me from whoever that was.

Moments later, all the lights came back on.

I looked to my right. Apartment 1020 was across from me. Tenth floor. I must have run faster than I thought. I found it difficult to catch my breath. My thoughts raced. Who the hell was that? How did he know my name?

None of it made any sense.

After a minute, I inched closer to the stairs and peered down, praying that nobody would be looking back up at me.

A man I had seen a few times inside the apartment building was walking up the stairs when I peered down. As he rounded the corner and up the flight of stairs I was on, he flashed me a smile and kept walking, a brown bag of groceries in his hand.

"Did you see anyone on your way up? A short man with pasty skin?"

The man shook his head and kept walking.

What the hell does that mean? Did I imagine him?

I collected myself a bit and slowly crept down two flights of stairs and knocked on Isabella's door.

"Sean," she said, quickly answering. "You look like you've seen a ghost."

Is that what he was? Only problem was that I didn't believe in ghosts. And he seemed much too real to make me even debate that with myself.

"Sorry to bother you again," I said, looking over my shoulder like a junkie on the lookout for cops. "But did the lights just go out in your apartment?" I swallowed and panted at the same time. "Like a blackout or something?"

She shook her head. "No. Why, did yours?"

I looked around the hall again.

"Are you alright, Sean? You don't look so good."

I turned back to Isabella. "So your lights didn't flicker or anything like that?"

She shook her head no.

I was sure of it now. I needed to get some help. I had to be going insane. What else could it have been?

Isabella said, "You sure you're alright?"

I looked around again. I then nodded. "I think I just need some sleep is all." I rubbed my eyes. The hangover wasn't doing me any favors, either. Had I permanently screwed up my brain? It was looking like a distinct possibility at that point. "Sorry about that," I said. "I'll talk to you later."

I left her and slowly walked back down towards my apartment, running past the fifth floor landing out of fear of a repeat visit from the sickly man. I just kept going when I reached my floor, all the way out of the building. I needed to see my shrink. And I needed to see him now.

7

Dr. Anders' office was three blocks from my apartment. I usually took my time on the walk, wishing the entire time that I was going anywhere but there. Not today. I needed to see him right away. I didn't have an appointment, but at the very least I would be somewhere that I considered safe for myself and for others. If I had gone off the reservation, at least I'd be in the right company.

I opted for the elevator rather than risk another run-in with that shady guy in the stairwell. In hindsight, it seemed like an even worse decision. At least with the stairs, I could run away if need be. In the elevator, I was stuck if he showed up again. And I couldn't think of anything I wanted less in this world than to see him again. Whoever that guy was, he made me feel dead inside. His voice, his appearance, his everything made my skin want to turn inside out to hide from him.

I pushed the mostly-glass door of Dr. Anders' office open and walked into the empty waiting room, heading directly up to the front. I tapped quickly and quietly on the sliding glass window and was happy to see the familiar face of Phyllis behind it. She was a pretty woman in her late sixties. She was a very to-the-point type of person. It was one of the reasons I actually liked her as opposed to being disgusted by her, like the rest of the people in my life. Plus, she had a great personality. I envied her in a way.

She pushed open the sliding glass. "Hi, Sean." She then looked down at her appointment book. "Do you have an appointment today?"

"Hey, Phyllis. I really need to see the doctor. It's kind of an emergency."

How am I going to explain this?

"Okay. Give me a second," she said. She walked out from behind the reception area and into the waiting room. She knocked on the doctor's door. She then opened it slightly enough to poke her head in. "Sean O'Rourke is here to see you. He doesn't have an appointment, but says it's an emergency." Dr. Anders then said something I couldn't make out. Phyllis then opened the door fully. "You can go on in, Sean."

"Thanks, Phyllis." I brushed past her and into Dr. Anders' office.

"Is everything alright, Sean?" Dr. Anders asked as I walked in. He knew me better than most people. I wasn't sure if that was a good or a bad thing. But at that moment, it was the only thing I had.

"Not really," I said. "I think I'm losing my mind."

Dr. Anders stood from behind his desk and walked over to the familiar area with two couches and a chair. "Care to sit?" he asked, motioning.

"Thanks," I said, taking a seat in my usual spot on the couch against the wall. I rubbed my knees nervously and rocked in place a bit. That was surely what a crazy person does. I'd seen it in movies. Next, I'd start talking to myself out loud. Then I wondered if I was already doing that but didn't notice.

"Relax, Sean. Remember, there is no judgment here."

"I can't," I said. "Relax, that is. Something's going on with me. And it's getting worse."

"Can you elaborate on what that means to you?"

"I mean there is some freaky, losing-my-mind kind of shit going on right now. Pardon my French. It all started after I lost my job yesterday."

"I'm sorry to hear that, Sean. I know you

felt like that might happen at some point. But events like a job loss can force an already depressed person even further. It comes as no surprise to me that you feel lost, maybe a bit disconnected from the world since the event?"

Was that a question? I didn't know. Either way, he was right.

"It was a long time coming." I almost told him about my attempted suicide. But I felt like that would just cause more problems for me. I didn't need any more problems. I needed solutions. "Is there anything you can do for me?"

Dr. Anders wrote something down on his pad of paper and then looked to me. "I'm going to up the dose of your antidepressants. Sometimes a person requires a little extra help in times of need like this."

It's not what I went there for. But now that I knew what I didn't go there for, I was left wondering what it was that I wanted. To the best of my knowledge, Dr. Anders did not have a magic wand. He couldn't simply wish away what was going on with me. And I knew deep down that the increased meds weren't going to do anything. I couldn't explain it. I just knew that something wasn't right with me.

He scribbled a few more things on his pad

and then wrote me a new prescription.

"Give this to Phyllis on the way out so she can call it in for you. It's for 300 mg, double what you've been taking. It should help, Sean. And I want you to start taking it immediately."

I took the scrip. "Am I going insane?" I figured it couldn't hurt to be blunt. It wasn't out of the question, considering what had been going on.

"No, Sean. You're not going insane. You are suffering from an overload of stress. Losing your job on top of what you've already been through is something you simply can't deal with at the moment. While you see it as losing your job, your mind thinks of the ramifications: how will you pay your bills, buy food, pay for your car, and so on. You may not realize how much is actually pushing down on you until it's too late. That's why I want to increase your dosage, at least for the time being. It should help to stave off the immediacy of what you are currently feeling. Take the increase each day and I'll see you for our next appointment in," he flipped to the back of his notepad, "five days from now. If things haven't improved by then, we will consider alternatives. Okay?"

Alternatives?

As much as I didn't want him to, he was

making sense. And he did go to school for all those years to deal with people like me. Who was I to second guess him? The twenty beers last night probably didn't help me any. My brain was bound to revolt at some point. Now I sort of felt foolish. But that didn't explain what just happened in my apartment building.

"I saw someone," I blurted out. "He was a short, evil looking man. He said he would be watching me."

"When did you see this man?"

"Right before I came here."

The look on Dr. Anders' face changed a bit, somewhat more alarmed, but nothing shocking enough to make me think that I had just supplied the missing piece to my crazy puzzle. And he didn't press some hidden psychiatrist button to summon in the guys to put me in a straightjacket.

"Hallucinations are common during extremely stressful times, Sean. This is especially true for someone already suffering through bouts of depression and anxiety. There are chemicals in your brain that sometimes misfire when dealing with stressful points in one's life. It happens to the best of us." He smiled reassuringly, as if to let me know that I was still allowed to walk freely among the rest of society. "If the increased dosage does not work, then maybe we will switch your medication entirely. There are plenty on the market. They work in different ways with different people. We just need to find the correct combination for you."

His words were reassuring in a way. I liked that he had answers to my crazy statements. He wasn't judging me as harshly as I was judging myself. And I'm sure I wasn't the first person to come storming into his office with this kind of talk. I have to say, the quick visit did make me feel the slightest bit better. I think I made the right choice going to see him.

"Okay," I said. "Sorry about barging in like that. I was really freaking out."

"You never need to feel sorry, Sean. That's what I am here for. Now, I suggest you go home and get some rest if you can."

"I'll try," I said, standing from the couch. "Thanks again, doc."

I handed the prescription to Phyllis and left to go back home. I hoped with every tarnished fiber of my being that the sickly man was a onetime thing.

8

I could hear talking, muted and distant. I strained to listen. It felt like the more focused I was on trying to understand what they were saying, the less intelligent the words sounded. It reminded me of the teacher from Charlie Brown, muffled, but still meaningful in a way.

"Hello," I said, though it didn't feel like my lips moved. I know I heard my voice say it. That was strange.

I tried to open my eyes, but they refused to budge. I tried to stand, but I felt bound in a way, unable to move.

"Hello," I said again. "Who's there?"

The voices ignored me. It sounded like a man and maybe two women. Or maybe it was two men and a woman. I couldn't be sure. Their voices blended into a single murmur at times.

Then came the beeping; two beeps and then one long one. The pattern of beeps continued a few more times.

"Please answer me," I shouted, though again, my lips didn't move.

Then more talking, louder this time, almost

as if these voices were yelling.

Why were they yelling?

Then a jolt hit me like a bolt of lightning. One I felt permeate through every cell in my body.

9

I woke up covered in sweat and breathing hard, as if I had just run a marathon. I sat up in bed, knocking a couple of empty beer cans to the floor. I looked over to my alarm clock. 3:53 A.M.

The encounter with the sickly man in the hall had my mind going. I had to drink myself to sleep. It was the only way I could stop thinking about him. But that appeared to have its own adverse effects. The nightmare I was just in seemed so real, like more than a dream, as if I was living in it rather than visiting. I felt trapped, helpless to do anything but listen and hope it would soon end. It was probably just the beer talking, but it felt like more than that.

I tossed the sweaty sheets to the side and got out of bed. I walked across the dark apartment to the kitchen sink and poured myself a glass of stale-tasting water, which I emptied in a few gulps. Hunched over the sink, I tried to slow my breathing a bit. *It was just a bad dream,* I told myself. Even so, it was one hell of a bad dream.

I walked back across the sticky carpet and

over to the windows. I pushed aside the shade of the window closest to my bed and peeked outside. Triangles of frost filled the corners of the panes of glass, framed by chipping paint. More snow fell from the dark night sky, silhouetted in the streetlight's hazy glow on the far end of the alleyway below my window.

A sudden knock on my door made me jump back.

I looked at my clock again and then back to my door.

Who the hell is that?

A rush of panic set in. With the sickly man still on my mind, my first thought went to him. Was he behind that door? My heart raced out of control. I squeezed my eyes shut to stop the panic attack from springing out into the open. *Control your breathing. Deep breaths.* I tried to practice what Dr. Anders instructed me to do at times like this. I couldn't even get my breathing right.

The thing that really freaked me out is that nobody ever came to visit me, let alone at four in the morning.

Another knock.

I hesitantly walked the short distance to the door as quietly as I could, using only slow, well-placed footsteps. I inched closer to the door, staying to the right to avoid being seen through the bottom crack. I then reluctantly peered through the peephole, half expecting to see the sickly man's black eyes looking back.

Relief washed over me. It was Mack. I turned on the lights and opened the door.

Mack smiled.

"Mack. What the fuck? Do you know what time it is?"

"Indeed I do." He smiled at me. "May I come in?"

Mack was dressed in a black three-piece suit, with a bright red tie, and a tan overcoat – a far cry from his janitorial uniform. No hat though, despite the inclement weather. His shiny bald head gleamed beneath the overhead fluorescent lighting in the hall.

I stood aside and waved him into my apartment. "It's kind of early for a visit, don't you think?"

"Opportunity never sleeps, Sean."

Opportunity may not sleep, but I sure as hell needed some at that point. His arrival, even at that ungodly hour, may have been a blessing of sorts. I had questions, and he may be the only person that could answer them.

"Listen, Mack, some weird guy cornered me upstairs yesterday. He said you weren't who you said you were. Those were his words."

"I see," Mack said. He looked over to the couch. "Mind if I sit?"

"Yeah. Sure." I sat next to him.

Mack unbuttoned his jacket. "What was this man's name?"

"He didn't say." And I didn't care to know it.

"Well, what did he look like?"

"He was real skinny, sickly looking. Had thin, ratty hair. His skin was whiter than the snow outside." Scary as hell pretty much summed him up. It gave me goose bumps to even think about how he looked.

Mack sighed. "It's unfortunate that you had to make Drake's acquaintance."

I looked over, a bit shocked. "So you know him?" It wasn't the answer I was expecting, or really wanted to hear. I thought for sure that Mack would shrug it off. "Don't know who you're talking about," I thought he'd say. But he did know who I was talking about. And that made the sickly man real. He was no hallucination. I wanted to throw up. But I had nothing to give. So I began to pick at the skin around my thumb again. It hurt more this time, as it hadn't had enough time to heal.

"He's an old associate of mine," Mack said.

"You two worked together?" He certainly didn't seem like the kind of person Mack associated with. Not that I knew Mack well enough to truly make that assumption, but I honestly couldn't see that guy working with anyone.

"We parted ways due to," he paused, chewed on his bottom lip for a second or two, "differences. And he was none too happy about it." He then looked over at me. "Try to stay away from him if you can."

"Easier said than done, Mack." Now he was freaking me out even more. "That Drake guy found me," I said. "Trust me, I wish he hadn't. He gives me the creeps." Then I remembered. "He said he'd be watching me." I was starting to freak myself out. "Listen, Mack, I don't know if this is worth it to me – this whole job thing. I don't need some weirdo lurking in the shadows, following me everywhere I go. I already have enough problems."

Mack reached out and patted my knee reassuringly. "I'll take care of Drake," he said. "You needn't worry about him. The best thing you can do is to not afford him what he wants."

"That's all well and fine, Mack, but I am worried. He seems unstable. Like the kind of person that boils bunnies, if you know what I mean." And if someone didn't look stable to me, then they must have been flat out, lock them up, loony bin insane.

Mack said, "You just keep helping those in need, and I promise the rest will work itself out."

I was suicidal, so purposely putting myself in harm's way wasn't much of a stretch. But this Drake character chilled me to the bone.

"How can you possibly know if it will work itself out, Mack? How do I know he isn't waiting for me downstairs with a loaded gun, ready to blow my head clean off?"

"You don't," Mack said. "But that could happen to anyone at anytime and anywhere. We can't stop our lives from progressing out of fear, Sean. By doing so, you are only limiting yourself while the world passes you by." He then reached into his jacket pocket and removed a stack of hundreds. He didn't count them or split the pile. Instead, he placed the whole stack down on the coffee table in front of us. "That should take care of you for a bit," he said.

I looked at the stack in disbelief. It must

have been two or three inches high. More money in one place than I'd seen since my fifth grade trip to the State Treasury. Even without counting it, I could tell that it was more than I made in a month at Monutek.

"You trying to buy me off, Mack?"

He smiled. "Come now, Sean. I would think you'd be worth a lot more than that stack if I was."

And I would disagree entirely. My miserable life probably wasn't worth more than a pocketful of loose change.

The stack of cash in front of me didn't lessen the frightful feelings of the sickly man any. But Mack's reassurance that I was not in any danger did. I trusted him, despite my better judgment telling me to take a step back and reassess the entire strange situation I had gotten myself into.

"You sure I don't have to worry about him?" I said. "Drake was it?"

Mack nodded. "I'm positive," Mack said confidently. "But let me know if he approaches you again. Alright?"

I hesitantly nodded. Mack had a way about him. His confidence was contagious. His soothing voice and reassuring words calmed my frantic mind, something that I couldn't even do for myself. And even though the thought of Drake hadn't left my mind, I wasn't as worried about him as I was before Mack had arrived.

Feeling a bit relieved, I said "Want a beer?" It wasn't even four o'clock in the morning, but I was awake. And while the hangover that had become commonplace wasn't as bad as it usually was, I felt like this situation would be better handled with a slight buzz.

"Sure," Mack said with a smile.

I walked over to the fridge and removed two cold ones.

"Thanks," Mack said, tapping the top of the can and popping it open. He took a sip of the foam, then followed it by downing half of the can.

I opened my can as well and sat on my bed. "How did you know where I lived, anyway?"

Mack reached into his jacket pocket. "You dropped this at the bar." He held out my wallet.

"Thank you."

I had been so caught up in the past day's drama that I hadn't even realized I lost it. Not that it would have been a huge loss, with a crumpled five dollar bill, my expired driver's license, and an even more expired condom being its only contents.

With Mack's dark suit and long overcoat, I couldn't help but feel like I was talking to an FBI agent. But then that would mean I was working for the FBI in a roundabout way. And from what little I knew about them, the FBI wasn't much into charity work, or drunken idiots like myself.

"You said opportunity never sleeps."

Mack nodded.

"So what's this opportunity that couldn't wait until morning?"

"I'm assuming by now you've opened the envelope?" Mack asked.

I slowly brought the beer down from my mouth. "How did you know that?" I don't know why, but I looked around my apartment as if there were tiny cameras hidden everywhere, watching my every unimportant move. I was the epitome of a reality television star: talentless, mundane, and pitiful. Exactly what people enjoyed watching in order to feel better about themselves.

Mack said, "I knew you would open it."

"How did you know that?"

"Just a feeling," Mack said. "I have a good sense for people. And I was pretty sure I got a good read on you."

"Oh yeah," I said, almost laughing. Teams of doctors couldn't read me even after I willingly gave up information. How Mack thought he knew what made me tick after only a few drinks was beyond me. But I had to ask. "Care to enlighten me?"

Mack sipped his beer and then put the can down on the coffee table. He then sat up on the couch. "Deep down, you're a good man, Sean. You mean well. And you have a good heart. But you come off as rude to most people because they don't get you. They don't understand the mental toll it takes to constantly fight with your own thoughts, to be weighed down by seemingly everything you do. Most people have no clue how it feels to be submerged in despair day after day. You don't want to be that way. I know what I saw in your eyes. I've seen it before in others. And it's because of those things, and the fact that you told me you needed a job, that I knew you would eventually open up the envelope." He then picked his can of beer up and took a big gulp. "I knew you wouldn't let change go when it was staring you right in the face."

I watched Mack talk. I didn't know what made me more unsettled, the fact that Mack had the feelings he did, or the fact that his feelings were dead on.

I finished my beer and put the can down on the table. "So why are you here, Mack?" I began to feel like a puppet in his show.

"I'm here to give you a name," he said.

"Of who?"

"A person in need of your assistance."

"Is that how this whole thing works? I finish one and you give me another?"

"Somewhat," he said, in his usual cryptic manner. "Though you're not finished with your first task yet. Of that I can assure you. You'll know when it's finished."

I waited for another shiny green envelope, but Mack stayed still.

"Jake is across the street in the park," Mack said, finishing his beer. "Start by looking near the World War II monument."

The park?

The only people that were in the park during the winter were those who had no choice but to be there: the homeless. The same people that followed me down the street, begging for money. One homeless man even went as far as to call me a heartless bastard because I refused to give him money to buy booze with. Well, I assumed he wanted to buy booze with it anyway. And that was my booze money, damn it. He could find his own.

Mack stood. "Thanks for the beer," he said. "I'll be in touch." He then smiled and left my apartment as quickly as he came, gently closing the door behind him.

"Anytime, Mack," I said to an empty apartment. "Anytime."

The way I saw it, I had two choices at that point. I could go to bed or I could drink. I wasn't tired, however, and feared falling back to sleep and into the nightmare. I wasn't ready to handle whatever that was again. I walked over to the fridge and looked in. As it turned out, I was out of beer – Mack and I drank the last two. And I wasn't about to dig into the reserve stash. I wasn't desperate enough for those.

With those two options no longer feasible, a third decision echoed in my head. "His name is Jake," Mack's voice said, repeating in my thoughts.

I looked up from the floor and over to the window. I then dressed warm. It was bound to be cold at the park, especially in the wee hours of the winter morning.

10

I reluctantly walked from the relative warmth of my apartment building and into the unforgiving, snow-driven ugliness that was 4:30 in the morning. Snow scattered from the tops of the trees lining the road and danced with the howling gusts of wind.

I stood on the sidewalk for a moment and stared across the newly-plowed street. I considered turning around and nixing my little park journey before it began. But just like apartment 810, and in turn Isabella, I found myself strangely drawn across the street by something I couldn't really explain. It was more than an impulse, like I was being pushed in that direction, absent of thought.

Pulling my collar up, I made my way across the street and towards the park. I walked through the open black wrought-iron gates and trudged down the main path. The city didn't use its resources to clear the park in the winter, opting instead to wait for the spring and let Mother Nature take care of it naturally. The snow was thick and relatively untouched, up to my knees in places. And not having the foresight to wear boots that early in the morning, the cold seeped through my holey sneakers and made me regret my decision to cross the street almost instantly.

As I made my way further down the path, I heard someone cough from my right in between the gusts of wind. *Was that a cough*? I really couldn't tell. The sound was very faint and down a little from where I was.

I veered off the main path and down a small hill, careful of my footing, and towards the WWII monument Mack told me to look near. The monument was dedicated around the same time I moved into my apartment. I remember because the street was packed with cars, some double-parked, making it extremely difficult for the movers to unload my stuff from their truck. Not to mention the multi-gun salute that startled me into dropping the fish tank I was carrying at the time. I never knew a fish tank could shatter into so many pieces.

Another cough broke through the wintery gusts of wind as I made it to the monument. If it was a normal cough, I might not have heard it, but it was a hacking, deep cough; a sound not to be confused with any other.

Past the monument and off to the right burned a fire within an old, rusty barrel. The muted orange glow of the flame lit the area beneath the pedestrian bridge and created small glowing circles where it punched through the rusted-out holes in its side. Every time the wind blew, the fire flirted with being extinguished.

"Hello," I called out when I neared.

Not my first choice to yell out in the park during this hour, but it made the most sense at the time. I didn't know who I was dealing with. People didn't take too kindly to being snuck up on, especially those with nothing to lose. A prison term for murder would probably seem like a nice reprieve from being homeless in the middle of winter.

I heard a clang from beneath the bridge, like that of a bottle being kicked accidentally. I looked, but couldn't see anything aside from the barrel and its waning glow.

"Jake," I called out. "Is that you?"

What am I doing out here, I wondered as snow pelted the side of my face. The temperature seemed to drop a few degrees every minute or so.

Another gust of wind swept through the open area of the park that I stood in. I shielded my eyes from the fast-moving snow. The mini squall soon abated and I was able to look up. The first thing I saw when I did was his dirt-blotched face. The second thing I saw was his gloved fist as it hit me square in the forehead.

I went down hard on my back and deep into the snow. He then fell down on top of me, pinning my arms down beneath his knees.

He stared at me through aged, bloodshot eyes. "How do you know my name?"

"Jake?"

He eyed me for a moment with a scowl on his face. "Who wants to know?"

"My name's Sean. I'm here to help you." I had to stop saying that. It sounded cheesy and delusional, despite it being the truth.

Jake still stared at me. I could see the gears turning in his head. "Help me?" he said, gruffly. "I don't need no help." He then got off my chest and rose to his feet. He turned his back to me and walked towards the fire, leaving me on the ground like a piece of discarded trash.

I brought my left hand up and rubbed the spot where I'd been punched. I'd been hit before, a certain period of my life I tried to forget, so I knew a good punch when someone threw it. But in the past I knew when to expect it, so I could ready myself the best I could. His punch, however, came out of nowhere. Thankfully, having taken a few really good shots in the past, it felt as if Jake may have pulled his punch as more of a warning.

I got to my feet and brushed the snow off as best I could, shaking out small chunks that somehow found their way into the back of my shirt, chilling me even further.

Screw this guy. That was my first thought. He didn't want help, he shouldn't get it, especially after just cold cocking me. Yet I found myself drifting towards him, pushing through the snow and closer to the barrel.

Jake stood beside the barrel, warming his hands. He had a glove on his right hand, a mitten on his left. He wore layer upon layer of dirty, patchwork clothes. An old leather cap sat on his head, with furry earflaps flopping down on the sides. His wrinkled, weatherworn face was covered in a thick grey beard. For whatever reason, he looked exactly as I thought he would.

He looked up at me when I apparently got too close. "Get away from me," he said.

"Like I said, I'm here to help. That's all."

"I already told you, kid. I don't need no help. What are you, stupid or something?"

Walk across the street, give the homeless guys a couple bucks, and maybe talk for a bit. That's what I thought it would entail. But my whole quick and dirty plan assumed Jake wanted help. It was evident that was not the case. It also became clear that these *jobs* that Mack sends me on were not going to be easy.

"You mind?" I asked, nodding to the rock across the barrel from him.

He sneered and looked me over but said nothing.

I sat down while keeping my eyes on him. For all I knew, he was planning on lunging at me.

The fire wasn't strong, only a few thin branches and some newspaper burned within the barrel, but it felt good out there, surrounded by the miserable white stuff.

"You've got quite the punch." The cold refused to let the sting of his punch lessen, but it also numbed up my face so I was sure I couldn't feel its full effects yet.

Jake said nothing. He didn't even look at me. His wrinkled face glowed with an orange hue as he stared into the fire. A few minutes of silence went by before Jake reached into his layers of jackets and sweatshirts and removed a pint of what looked to be vodka. He unscrewed the cap and took back a long swig. No sooner had the liquor cleared his throat than he began to cough spastically. The same deep, bellowing cough I heard earlier.

I went over to him. "Are you alright?" I put my hand on his back.

He shrugged me off and walked away. "I'll be fine." He coughed a few more times before spitting to his right. A patch of blood crimsoned the snow. He downed another mouthful of vodka before hiding the bottle back amongst his clothes. He then turned around, with the same unpleasant look on his face. "How do you know my name?"

"Someone told me to help a man named Jake in the park?" I looked around. "And you're the only guy I can see, so I assumed you were Jake."

He walked past the barrel and over towards the rock I sat on. He stared down at me. "And who is this someone?" He coughed again. After the two or three violent hacks, he brought his hand to his mouth and wiped the bit of blood away with his dirty glove.

"Mack," I said matter-of-factly.

"Mack who?"

I never thought to ask Mack his last name. "I just know him as Mack."

Jake looked me up and down, sneering the whole time. "And why does this Mack character want you to help me?"

"That's what he does, err, rather, what I do for him. Help people."

"You some kind of charity worker or something?" Jake said. He walked past me and back to the barrel. He stood over it and peered in, warming his hands.

"I guess you could say that."

Jake grunted. "Well, I don't need yours or anyone else's help. I'm just fine how I am." He coughed again, this time for near a minute. This one must have hurt more than the others, as it dropped him to his knees. More blood trickled from his mouth. He tried to wipe it off, but gravity had plans of its own.

"You're clearly not well." I said, stating the obvious. I walked up beside him and put my hand on his back again. This time, he didn't shrug me off. I don't think he had the strength to. "Let me help you." He looked up at me. "Please," I said. "What do you have to lose?" For the first time in a long time, I felt the desire to actually help someone. Not only that, but I felt like I had the power to help him. The situation was foreign to us both. He was a stubborn old bastard - that much I had already figured out - but given his living conditions, I think I could cut him some slack on his attitude. It took one stubborn bastard to know another.

He coughed again, this one long and painful sounding. With my hand on his back, I felt his entire midsection heave in spasm, even through his thick clothing. Another gust of wind kicked up. It blew a wall of snow directly into us. The fire fluttered and fought to stay lit, but eventually lost its fight. Without the minimal warmth of its flame, the outside became unbearably harsh in a hurry. The true winter would not be fended off any longer. Its biting teeth were now free to do its worst.

"Come with me, Jake."

He looked at me through angry eyes. But I could see past it. He wanted help.

"Listen," I said. "I live right across the street." I pointed to my apartment building, though you couldn't see much of it through the squalls. "It's better than being out here." He looked up at me. "Right? Or do you truly enjoy being out in this shit?"

Just agree.

He finally – thankfully -- nodded and let me help him to his feet.

We trudged back up the hill and followed my footsteps back to the entrance. Even though he relented to come with me, he would not let me help him walk through the snow. I tried twice to help brace him. And twice he shrugged me off.

A plow truck scraped the street clean as we exited the gates of the park, revealing the yellow dividing line that had been snowed over since I crossed. The driver of the plow gawked at us as we emerged from the park, no doubt wondering why we were coming out of the park at this hour and in this weather.

We walked across the deserted street to my building. I held open the door and pushed Jake through as gently as I could. It ended up being more of a shove, but since I was cold and tired, he'd have to suffer through it.

As soon as the door slammed shut behind us, I felt relief. I didn't know what I was going to do now that we were out of the cold, but at that moment, it didn't matter. All that I worried about now was warming up. A numbness coursed through my feet that I hadn't felt since childhood, when the days of building snowmen and sledding for an entire day was nothing abnormal. Everything was simpler back then.

"I'm on the fourth floor." I said to Jake, nodding up the stairs. "Think you can make it?"

"Do I look like some kind of damn cripple

to you?" He pushed past me and started up the stairs.

After you. He was the definition of a curmudgeon.

Jake stopped at the top of the fourth floor landing. He looked back as I climbed the last few steps until I was on even footing with him.

"It's down the hall," I said, walking past him.

He followed.

I fumbled for my keys. The tingling in my hands felt like they were almost burning, which I knew was only the blood starting to circulate again now that we were out of the cold.

I opened the door. Jake followed me in.

"Can I get you something warm to drink?" I asked before I even looked to see if I had something warm to drink. I probably had some cocoa somewhere. Then again, if cocoa expired, I didn't have anything.

"I've got something warm right here." He patted his coat where he put the vodka back. "Wouldn't mind something to chase it with, though."

If that made him happy, so be it. I opened the fridge door and looked in. A jar of pickle spears sat off to the right. The same jar of pickles I'd had for over two years. I don't' know why I kept them. They'd become sort of a sad staple in my fridge. Besides that, there was a carton of pizza that had been in there for a few weeks. Not surprisingly, I was too lazy to throw it out.

And as I discovered before going to gather Jake, I was out of beer. All I had left was the reserve stash on the bottom shelf, the super-cheap, I'm-already-drunk-so-what-the-hell beer. I didn't even consider it beer. It was more of an emergency extension for a night I wanted to last a bit longer.

"Sorry," I said, my head still inside the refrigerator. "All I have is the cheap stuff."

Jake grunted again. "What kind?"

I stood up and looked back. "What?"

"Are you deaf?" Jake coughed again but not as bad as before. "I asked you what kind of beer you have."

"Does it matter?"

"I don't drink none of that foreign crap."

A bum with a refined pallet, that's who I had just dragged off the street. *Great.*

"It's American beer." I took a can out of the fridge and handed it to him. "Just not good American beer."

He eyed it discriminately before popping

the top and taking a big gulp. He followed that with a swig of his vodka and another large gulp of the beer.

"Nice place," Jake said, looking around. "Messy though." He looked back to me. "You're kind of a slob, huh?" He walked over to the window and peered out. "And your view sucks." He then looked down at the few pictures I had in my apartment. "This your mother?" Jake asked. He held the largest framed picture I had in his hand.

While I had her picture there to look at, I rarely thought about it. Not because I didn't want to, but because she was one of the few woman that I unequivocally loved in this world. And when I thought about her, about her passing, it brought the pain associated with her leaving me to the forefront – pain I couldn't handle. But I never once thought about putting it away. I wanted to always remember her spirit and love.

"Can you put that down please?" I asked.

Jake must have sensed my uneasiness, as he didn't blurt out a smartass remark. He put the picture down and walked over to the couch, plopping himself down. He coughed again, this time following it up with the rest of his beer.

He jiggled the empty can. "Have any more of these?"

"Help yourself," I said on my way across the room. "They're in the bottom drawer of the fridge."

I walked into the bathroom and shut the door. I sat on the toilet for a few minutes with my head in my hands. I think I had gotten myself in over my head. I was obviously ill-equipped to handle this emotionally. It was hard enough dealing with my own broken self, let alone someone else. I'd give Jake a place to sleep tonight and then figure out where to take this tomorrow.

I stood from the toilet and looked in the mirror. I was an absolute mess. I looked worse than Jake and I didn't have nearly the same excuses he had. But there wasn't time for me and my appearance. For reasons I still couldn't really wrap my head around, I now had other people to take care of. So, I took a deep breath and opened the bathroom door.

"Listen, Jake…"

Jake's snoring cut me short. He was fast asleep on the couch. A second empty beer can sat on the table to his left. Even my less-than-warm apartment must have felt like a tropical island, considering what he was used to. I walked over to the couch, removed the blanket from the floor, and covered him up. At least one of us could find some sleep.

11

With little hope of falling asleep naturally, the emergency beers were called upon to help. I downed one after another until I knew my mind could no longer continually pose questions that I didn't have the answers to. I dreamt of my Mother during that short rest. Jake picking up her picture must have sparked something inside me. I didn't dream of her for long, but just enough to remember how terribly I missed her still to this day. She was the one person in this horrid world that had unequivocally protected me. But then she was ripped from my life by cancer when I needed her the most, leaving me with an emotional hole that would never be filled, leaving me to face the monster alone.

The sound of the shower running woke me.

I opened my eyes and looked around. My pants were crumpled to the side of my bed atop my shoes. I must have passed out while getting undressed as I still wore my sweatshirt, boxers, and socks. A small puddle of drool gathered to the side of my face, wetting the pillow in what looked like the shape of Alaska. I'd take that over what I had been waking up to recently.

The blanket was still on the couch, but Jake was not. For better or worse, he appeared to be taking a shower.

I pushed myself off the bed, knocking the empties to the floor as I did.

My always present headache made itself known. And beneath the headache lurked my depression. Sometimes I could swear it was talking to me, leading me to hate myself and my life, willing me to give in fully to its dark desires. But I had given in, that's the thing. My depression had won. But it continued to beat me while I was down, unrelenting and depravedly mean.

Jake walked out of the bathroom, a towel thankfully wrapped around his waist and another slung over his shoulders. With his hat off, Jake's ring of hair frizzled in a multitude of different directions around the center bald spot, like an ocean of branches and twigs surrounding a desolate island.

"Thanks for the shower, kid," he said. He walked over to the fridge, opened it, and looked back at me. "Looks like you were busy after I conked out."

I went to speak, but my mouth was as dry as the desert.

He removed the last beer in the fridge. "You mind?"

I waved him on. I wanted nothing to do with that, or any other beer at that moment.

He opened the can and took a long pull. He then held the can out and looked at it admirably. "Haven't had a cold beer in years," he said. "I usually stick to the hard stuff. Gets me drunk quicker and tends to keep me warm." He laughed. The laugh soon turned into the same coughing fit he had only hours ago. The coughing ended quicker this time, with no blood. Maybe the warmth did him some good.

He sat on the couch and put his legs up on the coffee table.

I shut my eyes instinctively. "Do you mind?" I asked Jake. The gaping view of his privates was something I never wanted to see, let alone first thing in the morning. I felt it searing, a new, unwanted memory.

Jake rolled his eyes. "Sorry about that." He stood up and walked over to the bathroom.

"There's an extra razor in there if you want."

Jake looked back. "Nah," he said, stroking

his mangy beard. "I've grown accustomed to it. It helps keep me warm."

I pushed myself off the bed and stood still for a moment to gather my balance. I then walked over to the windows and looked out to find it still snowing. It was thankfully no more than a flurry, probably wouldn't stick, but it still sucked to see. I hated the winter and everything it brought with it.

"So," I said, turning to Jake. "How can I help you, Jake?"

Jake walked out of the bathroom. He had put his grungy pants back on, but was still covered in my blue and white towel around his shoulders.

"Like I said to you last night, I don't need no help." He seemed adamant about that. "But I do appreciate you lending me your couch last night, kid. I forgot what that felt like." He seemed to get lost in his own words, staring off at nothing for a few seconds.

"Do you have any family?" I asked.

The semi-smile on Jake's face vanished. He looked over at me. "Don't ask me about stuff I don't want to talk about."

"How am I supposed to know what you want to talk about?"

"Let's just assume I don't want to talk

about nothing," he said. "Okay?"

Jake looked at me with the most serious of faces. He may have been a drunken homeless man that was rough around the edges, but he was clearly human beneath all that grime. I sensed that I was getting somewhere. But as soon as I got there, the door slammed shut. I felt like I shouldn't push the issue.

"Okay, okay," I said. "Sorry I brought it up."

He eyed me another minute and then went back into the bathroom to finish getting dressed. A few minutes later, he walked out, looking the same as he did last night, albeit a bit cleaner.

"Well, kid, I gotta get going. Things to do, people to see." He laughed again, followed by another fit of coughs. This time, he wasn't so lucky as to avoid the blood.

I had to close my eyes. My headache left me no choice. *Why did I constantly do this to myself*? But I couldn't just let him run off like that. "Jake, there's a clinic a couple blocks from here. Let me take you there to get looked at." I opened my eyes and waited for his answer.

Jake opened my apartment door. "No need. I'll stop by my doctor's office," he coughed again, "on the way to my mansion."

He stepped into the hall. "See ya kid," he said as the door closed behind him.

Like I had been doing a lot of lately, I trusted my instincts and hurried across my living room and opened my apartment door. I stepped into the hall and over to the staircase. I looked down, but Jake was already out of sight.

"Sean?"

I turned to find Isabella standing there, as if she had just appeared. She had her hand over her mouth, like a pubescent girl covering her first pimple.

"Is everything alright?" I said. I could tell just by her mannerisms that she wasn't expecting to talk to anyone on her way out. She seemed surprised and a bit unnerved to see me.

"Everything's fine," she said. She smiled, but I could only see her left dimple with her hand blocking the entire right side. "Maybe I should be asking if you're okay, Sean." She looked me over.

I waved her off as if I was fine. "Just had a little too much to drink last night, that's all."

She looked at me in horror and took a step back. Her whole demeanor changed. "I have to go." She walked past me and hurriedly down the stairs.

"Isabella, wait," I shouted. "What did I say?"

But she soon disappeared out of sight down the staircase, just as Jake had.

I walked the few steps back into my apartment. My life was quickly becoming a zoo. Two strangers, people I had just met the day before, couldn't get away from me fast enough. I was starting to feel like there was no one on the planet who felt like being with me. And these were people with supposed problems. What did that say about me?

"Airing out your delicates?"

I turned to find Mack standing in my doorway, smiling.

It was like Grand Central Station all of a sudden.

I looked down and shook my head. I was in such a rush to catch Jake that I hadn't remembered I was only half dressed. No wonder Isabella rushed past me. Not only was I the wandering weirdo of the apartment complex, but I was now also the perverted flasher. It was a great combination for someone who already thought so highly of himself.

Mack walked into the apartment and stood next to me. "How are you coming along,

Sean?"

I went over and put on my jeans as quickly as I could. "I don't really know, Mack. If I had to guess, I'd say not very well."

He looked at me, silent, and waited for me to elaborate. But the thing was I didn't know how to. I didn't know what it took to complete these tasks. So how I was *coming along* was beyond me. I was a kid to Jake and a pervert to Isabella.

"What does it take, Mack?"

He looked at me, expressionless.

"What do I have to do to help these people?"

"That's for you to decide, Sean." Mack put his hand on my shoulder. "But what I can tell you is to trust your instincts. Go with what they're telling you to do."

I had trusted my instincts. That's exactly what got me in the position I was in.

"So what's up, Mack? What brings you to my stately abode?"

"I have to go away," Mack said. "I have a short business trip I need to take. So you'll be on your own for a bit."

"What should I do in the meantime?"

"Keep at it," Mack said with a smile. "I promise you'll find what you're looking for eventually."

"But I don't know what I'm looking for. That's the problem."

Mack smiled and patted me on the back. "If these problems were easy to fix, you wouldn't be the one fixing them. Right?"

"I guess so," I said reluctantly. "But I have been going on instinct and it's gotten me nowhere so far. Jake just left. He'd apparently prefer to be outside in the cold, shitty weather rather than locked in this apartment with me. And Isabella," I laughed in disgust of myself. "Well, she just saw me standing in the middle of the hallway with no pants on. So as you can probably assume, things aren't going as I would like them to."

Mack smiled. "They never do, Sean. But that's life, unpredictable as the day is long. It's what you do with that unpredictability that defines you." He opened my apartment door and stood in the doorway. "Just keep chipping away at it. Eventually, you will find out that you are better at this than you think you are."

Like I had a choice. "Okay, Mack," I said. "But I can't promise this is going to work out the way you envisioned it."

"All I can ask is that you try," Mack said, taking another step out of my apartment and into the hallway. "I'll see you soon, Sean." He then closed the door behind him.

Left alone with my own thoughts, I wasted no time in going back to bed to try and avoid them.

12

Again, I was surrounded by darkness. And again, I felt as if I couldn't move. I felt bound entirely, as if I had been glued down, wherever I was. Spurts of shouting came from my right and then faded to my left, a man, or maybe it was a woman. It was too hard to tell. The voices sounded submerged and distant. I went to speak but I couldn't. But unlike the last time, my mouth felt as if it was wide open rather than sealed shut. And then a sudden jolt, stronger than the one in the previous nightmare, coursed through me from my toes up to my fingers, shooting me out of whatever that was.

I opened my eyes. My breathing was heavy and sporadic. I brought my hands up to my head and took a moment to collect myself. Whatever was going on with me seemed to be getting worse.

"Sean." I heard from the other side of my door. It was Isabella. "Are you home?"

She knocked. "Sean?"

All too accustomed to waking in the middle of the night lately, I jumped out of bed and threw on some pajama pants and a t-shirt.

I double checked to make sure I actually put on my pants. Once could be considered a mistake. But doing it twice was something I'd rather not put myself through. I then hurried over to the door. I didn't bother looking through the peephole. Her soft and pleasing voice was unmistakable.

When I opened the door, I was met with a sight not completely uncommon to me, though I wished it was. Isabella stood there shaking, bleeding from her nose, with the makings of a shiner on her right eye. I instantly became angry, livid almost. Images of my mother flashed in front of my eyes, bruised, beaten, and helpless.

"What happened, Isabella?"

"Can I come in?"

"Of course." I couldn't get out of the way fast enough.

She walked past me and over to the couch. I turned on the light and sat beside her. I went to prod, to find out what the hell happened, but before I could she leaned into me, buried her head into my shoulder, and started to cry. She cried hard, to a point where she almost couldn't catch her breath. I sat there silently and let it be, holding her as compassionately as I could without giving her the wrong impression. It was best to let her empty whatever emotions needed to come out.

A few minutes passed before she looked up. She wiped her eyes. "I'm sorry," she said. "I had nowhere else to go."

I rubbed her back. "It's okay," I said. "I'm glad you came to me." There was a flood of words wanting to come out, but I kept them back. Comforting someone wasn't something I was used to. I thought for sure after our indecent encounter in the hallway that we would never speak again, so I was glad to see her. Just not under these circumstances.

"I'm so sorry," she said, wiping my shirt with her hand. "Look what I did."

I looked down to see the smear of blood from her nose stretching across my shirt.

"Please. Stop saying that. You have nothing to be sorry about," I said. The shirt was well past its prime. Probably best I got rid of it, anyway. "What happened to you, Isabella? Who did this?" I asked, walking to the bathroom and returning with a roll of toilet paper. I wasn't civilized enough to have tissues like the rest of the world.

She shook her head very softly, almost reluctantly. A few more tears dripped from her eyes and down her cheeks. "It was just a fight," she said. "It was my fault." She turned away from me and forced more tears out. "I shouldn't have been so demanding."

A sickening feeling filled my stomach. More images of my mother whipped by my eyes. Not the same ones I saw when I was lucky enough to fall into a deep sleep, but rather those images I tried not to remember, images of the after effects from battles with my Father, the monster. The bruises on her face were an unforgettable scar on my memories.

I burned red with rage from within. How could someone do this to Isabella? I'd known her for only hours, yet I felt as if she was my own blood.

Isabella touched my arm. "Don't," she said. "Please."

I turned to her with fire in my eyes.

"Don't go up there, Sean."

"But, Isabella."

"Please," she begged. "I didn't come down here for that. I just--" She sobbed harder and looked away.

I sat silently and let her gather her thoughts. I wanted to ease her pain, tell her that everything would be alright. I didn't know that, though. I wanted to afford her the lie, regardless. But I felt like that would be a disservice to the moment.

She turned back. "It's just that the other day you said you came up to help me." She looked away bashfully. "And I guess I could just use some help right now. But running upstairs," she said, looking back at me and gently touching my hand, "while noble of you, is not what I need right now. It would just make matters worse."

Part of me was happy to hear her say that. I wanted to go up to the eighth floor, driven by an anger that had been building up over the years, but I knew it would do little for me in a real fight. Aside from picking on smallish nine-year old Timmy Caldwell when I was thirteen, I hadn't really been in a fight. I'd been on the receiving end of many a beating, but never really a fight. I would most likely get the crap kicked out of me if I went to her apartment. But someone needed to stick up for her. She was the same as my mother was, always blaming herself for what the monster did. It was never the abuser's fault in their eyes.

"Okay, Isabella," I said. "I won't go up there." Part of me was relieved, while the other part hated the chicken shit I secretly was.

"Please promise me, Sean."

I nodded.

"Say it," she said. "Please. I need to hear you say it. You don't know what he's capable of. I don't want you to get hurt."

The guy buried deep inside me wanted to spray machismo all over her, to scoff at the fact that I could get hurt in the first place. But I was much less of a man than I should have been, and that side of me was buried far too deep beneath the blackness to ever be seen.

"I promise, Isabella." But then I couldn't help myself. "But why do you stay with him if he does this to you?" I was prying now, but I felt as if I no longer had a choice. She came to me. I thought I had the right to ask, if only for her safety.

She looked at me through her watery eyes. Sadness filled every tear. "Sam used to be a good man, back when we first met. But after I broke off the engagement--" She started to tear up again and shook her head, trying not to cry. "It's my fault he's like this now."

"You were engaged?"

Isabella nodded. "A little over a year ago."

"If that's no longer the case, then why are you still together?" I knew I went too far over the invisible line, but at that point it didn't really matter. She was opening up to me. And the moment begged for me to step up.

"I needed more time," she said. "But it's not like I didn't love him anymore. I did. I really did. It just didn't feel right." She unrolled a bit of the toilet paper from the roll and dabbed the blood on her upper lip. "He wasn't very happy with my decision." She wiped her eyes and sniffled. "So we kept living together until I was ready. I really thought all I needed was a bit of time. I kept waiting to change my mind, for the time to feel right, but it never did. I began to think I was afraid of marriage, of commitment. But as time went by, I came to grips with the fact that I wasn't in love with him anymore. But how do you tell someone that?"

Her nose stopped bleeding, most of it on my t-shirt. And now that I sat across from her, it was easy to spot five or so new bruises. I could only imagine what her clothes hid. Anger again seethed within me.

She then laughed nervously. "But he really is a good man."

"He's not a good man, Isabella. Anyone that could do this to you is a spineless dick. You shouldn't protect him or what he's done to you. It's not right. There is no acceptable excuse for this."

I was riling myself up. Thoughts of my

father hitting my mother slammed into me. I wanted to punch something that couldn't punch back, the wall, the table, anything at that moment to release my building rage.

Isabella began to cry again, softly.

"I'm sorry," I said. "I, I, shouldn't have said that." I overstepped my bounds.

Idiot.

"It's nothing you said." She looked away, towards the other side of my apartment. Her cheeks glistened with tears. "You're right, Sean. He has become a monster. More so since I broke off the engagement. But this isn't who he always was. He's turned into a hateful drunk who can't accept that life changes." She looked away, finally with a bit of anger in her eyes. "So he takes it out on me."

I went to speak but nothing came out. Were there correct words for this type of situation? I sure as hell didn't know.

Then Isabella said, "And that's why I rushed past you yesterday in the hall. You said you'd been drinking and, it's just." She brought her hands up to her eyes and wept some more.

So it wasn't the fact that I was standing in the hall in my boxers. I didn't know whether to laugh or join her in crying.

"Isabella, I can promise you I'm nothing like him. I would never..."

"I know, Sean. " She smiled sweetly. "But I've seen firsthand what alcoholism can do." She held up her arm and rolled up her sleeve. "This is just one of the many side effects." She had a large gauze strip wrapped around her arm. A small red line stained it in the middle.

"What happened there?"

She looked to the wound and then back at me. "This is what happened when I tried to defend myself. I grabbed a knife to keep him back, but he lunged and grabbed it from me. When he did, the knife slipped and cut my arm. It was an accident. And he begged me to forgive him. I know he didn't mean to cut me. But he was the one that put me in a position to be cut in the first place." She clenched her jaw tight and looked away. "God, why am I so stupid?" She then looked back. "So I put some gauze on the cut and left the apartment. That was about thirty minutes ago."

This was far more serious than I thought. Abuse was one terrible thing. Flirting with dangerous, possibly life-ending weapons was a completely different and far more horrible one. Isabella had only been in my apartment for ten or so minutes, though.

"Where did you go before you came here?"

"I sat on the steps outside your door and cried. I almost didn't knock."

"I'm glad you did."

She smiled. "So am I, Sean."

I couldn't get the thought of this drunk guy with a knife out of my head. I didn't know what he looked like, but I pictured a giant of a man. "I think you should go to the police, Isabella. What happened is pretty serious."

"I know I should. He didn't mean it, though. And I was the one that pulled the knife in the first place."

"But it was in self-defense."

"I know." She touched my hand gently again. "Trust me, I know. But he'll sleep it off and maybe we can work it out when he wakes up."

"Stay here," I blurted out. "You can have the bed. I'll sleep on the couch." Then I thought about my crusty pillow and the fact that I hadn't washed my sheets in too long. "Actually, you have the couch. It's more comfortable." It was easier to lie than to admit how disgusting I was.

"That's so sweet of you, Sean." She leaned in and kissed my cheek, directly above my beard. Her lips were soft, like flower petals.

Her hair smelled like lavender. "But if I stayed here, it would only create new problems," she said. "I think it's best that I deal with it when the time is right. I told him tonight that I was leaving if he didn't quit drinking tomorrow. I know I shouldn't give him another chance, but some part of me won't let go of what we had, even though it's something we'll never get back. Something I don't want back. But I can't help but to feel guilty for pushing him to become who he is now."

In a strange way, I understood what she was getting at. Despite me hating my Father, there was a point in my life when I thought he could revert back to the man I knew before my Mother passed and not the monster he had become in her final years. Of course, those thoughts were as misguided as Isabella's. But it wasn't my place to tell her that.

"Thank you," Isabella said, "for being here for me." She wiped her eyes. She then gently stroked my cheek. She took a deep breath and exhaled it. "It's what I needed."

"Do you think it's safe to go back up there?" Letting her leave to go back upstairs, to the scene of the crime, went against my better judgment. But who was I to tell a grown woman her business?

"It's fine," she said. She had stopped crying, and her bloody nose had ceased dripping. "He's probably passed out drunk by now. Don't worry, Sean. I'll be okay. He knows he went too far."

"Are you sure?"

She nodded. She then stood and gave me a big hug. It felt so good I wished she'd never let go. She then walked over to the door, opened it, and looked into the hall. "I'll see you soon." She then left me alone in my apartment.

As a man, I should have gone upstairs, despite her pleading with me not to. I should have busted down her door and tossed him out the window. To be honest, I was scared of the confrontation, of becoming less of a man than I already was. It was a risk I was willing to take for Isabella.

Mack sent me to Isabella to help her and when she needed it the most, I couldn't bring myself to do it. Sure, I was there for her emotionally, but considering who I was, it couldn't have been all that much. For all I knew, her monster might not be passed out. He could be hitting her in the face again, making her bleed, tormenting her more than he could ever know. Or he could be doing much, much worse.

People tend to fear the monsters that hide in the dark. But coming from experience, what they should fear more are the ones that prey out in the open.

13

The image of Isabella, beaten and bruised, was one that haunted me until the sun came up. A few times during the night, I heard something that sounded like a scream. Once I was so sure of it, I had hopped out of bed and ran for the door. I made it halfway before realizing it was nothing more than a police car with its sirens on. I knew if Isabella had screamed, I wouldn't have heard her from where I was, no matter what my mind insisted. But it didn't stop the thoughts from coming. It was a torturous night I inflicted on myself, all because of my own inaction.

She asked me not to go upstairs. But did she really mean it? It was so frustrating to never know if I should trust my thoughts, feelings, or instincts. I could never be sure if what I was doing was the correct thing, because I didn't know what the correct thing was. Self-doubt was a powerfully affective tool at keeping me dwelling in the darkness.

I reached to my right, over to the window closest to my bed, and pulled up the shade. Sunlight bathed the inside of my apartment. I don't know what surprised me more, the fact that it wasn't snowing, or that I somehow, someway, lacked my usual morning headache. And because of that, I didn't feel as miserable as I usually did, though I did have to remind myself that the day had just started. There was plenty of time for me to fuck it up royally.

I figured I would use the opportunity to get out of my cramped and cluttered apartment. I walked the few blocks from my apartment to Larry's Coffee House and grabbed two extra-large Columbian blends, one for me and one for Jake. If I couldn't fix what troubled Isabella, then I might as well work on Jake. I knew his problem, whatever it was, would be more difficult if not impossible to fix, because he already told me he didn't want any help. Stubbornness was a tough shell to crack. At least Isabella wanted some kind of help, even though I provided little of it. But with her, I could see the problem, just not the solution. With Jake, I was in the dark entirely. And I sensed it was going to be an uphill battle the whole way.

As I trudged along the sidewalk, fighting against the flow of pedestrian traffic, the peculiarity of what I was doing couldn't be overlooked. So far, I had done what I was asked to do by Mack. A combination of the need for money and a lack of motivation to do anything else had brought me to this point. But there I was, in the cold, going into the desolate park to try and coax a problem out of a homeless man who didn't want any of it. I wouldn't have been surprised to see a television crew jump out from behind the nearest tree and tell me I was on some hidden camera show. It would have been more believable than my reality.

I took a sip of my coffee, which had already cooled off in the frigid February air, and once again walked through the iron gates at the park's entrance. My footprints from the other night were for the most part erased, but I knew which way to go. If I could navigate the unplowed path in the dark, I could certainly do it during the day. Having two coffees, one in each hand, made my balancing act that much more difficult, but I managed to exit the path and go off to the right towards the monument.

Carefully traversing the small hill, I soon reached the barrel from the other night. I looked in to find a small pile of ashes beneath some snow. To the pile's right was Jake's vodka bottle. I reached out. The barrel was cold to the touch. I was now worried more about Jake. I remembered how cold it got when the fire had blown out.

I looked up from the barrel and squinted into the blindingly bright, snow covered park. The trees were heavy with snow, making them look like white lollipops that had fallen stick first from the sky. Some of the younger ones leaned to either direction, with the smallest of them actually bending to gently kiss the ground.

I walked a bit further in, towards the arching bridge that spanned the jogger's path. Beneath the bridge was a lump. I looked closer and saw a pair of boots attached to the lump. Jake's boots. I hurriedly walked towards the bridge, pushing as fast as I could through the snow.

"Jake," I said, staring down at him. His back was facing me. He was covered in a dirty blanket up to his chin. His leather cap adorned his head.

I put the coffees down and nudged his arm. *This guy can sleep through anything.* "Jake," I said. "Don't go getting all mad at me. I just figured you could use a coffee."

Still nothing.

I climbed over him and to the other side. His eyes were closed. His face was dark red where his beard wasn't. I would have thought him dead had it not been for the very slight movement of the blanket as he breathed.

"Wake up, Jake."

His eyes cracked open, slits at first, then a tiny bit more. He was expressionless, but I could tell he was in pain. Not the kind of pain that made a person scream or wince, but the numbing kind of pain felt after they've endured too much. It was the look of a person who had given up. A look I'd seen in the mirror more than once.

I was relieved not only that he was alive, but that I wouldn't have the weight of his death on my shoulders.

Stop being selfish. This isn't about you.

I knew I shouldn't have let him go the other night. Relief was quickly replaced by anxiety. What was I supposed to do now?

The area around Jake's mouth was caked with dried blood.

"Come on, Jake." I said, trying to pry him off the cold ground. "I have to get you some help."

He didn't argue. That alone alarmed me. He also didn't move. It quickly became apparent that I couldn't lift him by myself. That much I knew. He outweighed me by more than fifty pounds and dragging him through the knee-high snow wasn't an option.

I eased him back down. "I'll be right back, Jake. Just hang on."

I reached for my cell. *Dammit*. I had left it in the apartment. I could go back and get it, but I didn't know how long Jake had. He didn't look good.

I turned and ran. It felt like my feet never hit the ground, I was moving so fast. I strode purposefully until reaching the park's entrance.

"Excuse me," I said to a woman in a fur coat as she walked by the park's gate.

She stopped but kept her distance from me.

"Can I use your phone?" I tried to catch my breath, gasping in between my sentences. "It's an emergency."

She looked me up and down and then sneered. "Sorry. I don't have a phone." That's all she said before turning and walking away.

Bitch.

I ran up to another man who was talking on his cell phone by a bus stop. At least he couldn't use the same excuse.

He saw me coming and stopped and looked at me like I had two heads. I put my hands on my knees and looked up at him. "It's an emergency," I said, pointing to his phone. "Can I please use your phone?" I was so lightheaded now I thought I'd be joining Jake on the ground any second. Exercise of any kind was not my thing.

"I'll have to call you back," the man said, hanging up his call. "You going to be alright, buddy?"

I nodded. "Yes," I said. "I'll be fine. But a friend of mine needs help in the park. I need to call an ambulance."

The man nodded and wasted no time. He quickly dialed 9-1-1. "Ya, hi," he said as the operator picked up his call. "We need an ambulance at Veteran's Park."

He looked to me and moved the phone from his mouth. "She wants to know what the emergency is?"

I shook my head. I didn't know exactly. "I think he's dying," I said, trying to catch my breath again. I gulped. "Homeless man named Jake. Tell them to hurry."

The man relayed my message and then quickly hung up.

"They're sending an ambulance," he said.

I nodded. Still lightheaded, I said "Thank you."

I went running back, despite my desire to

collapse into the snow from exhaustion. I reached Jake and went back to the ground by his side. He was more alert now, but far from okay.

"Help's on the way," I said to him.

Jake had managed to roll onto his back. A fresh, thin creek of blood flowed down his cheek. He went to speak, but broke into a fit of coughing that forced him to heave in pain. The coughing subsided, but the pain in his face did not.

"I know," I said. "You don't need help. But it's coming anyway." I just hoped it got there in time.

Jake grinned and closed his eyes.

The ambulance's siren cut through the howl of the wind a few minutes later. It grew louder until arriving at the front entrance. Two paramedics followed by a cop made their way to us beneath the bridge, following the only footsteps to be seen. The amount of snow slowed them down considerably, but they hurried nonetheless.

I turned to them. "His name is Jake. I don't know what's wrong with him." I then stood and moved out of their way.

The first paramedic nodded. "Can you hear me, Jake?" he asked.

Jake opened his eyes a bit and nodded so slightly that even those with perfect vision could have missed it. But the paramedic's trained eye saw it. "Okay, good. How long have you been out here, Jake?" The paramedic removed a stethoscope from his orange medical box. He put them on and reached into Jake's clothing, putting the cold circle to Jake's chest, and listened.

Jake didn't answer. I don't think he could even if he wanted to.

The paramedic turned to his partner. "We have to move him now."

The second paramedic nodded and went to the other side of Jake with a flat stretcher and put it down. He then grabbed Jake's feet while the first paramedic grabbed him by the shoulders.

"One, two, three, lift," the first paramedic said. They quickly transferred Jake to the board.

"What can I do to help?" I asked. I felt as helpless as always.

"Calling for help was the right thing to do," the first paramedic said. "We'll take it from here."

They strapped him down, carefully but quickly. This was clearly not their first time doing it.

I noticed the cop inch up a bit closer to me out of the corner of my eye. "How do you know him?" he asked.

The answer to that question would no doubt lead to more questions. I could always tell him the truth: that I met some guy on a roof when I was trying to kill myself, only to be offered the job of helping people fix their problems. That would probably go over real well. I'm sure they'd believe me.

"I don't know him," I said. A lie seemed less complicated. "I just found him like this." But I obviously hadn't thought my spontaneous lie out.

The cop looked at me funny. "Why were you out here in the first place? You enjoy leisurely strolls in the snow?"

I shook my head. "No, no, it's nothing like that." I was getting flustered. "Does it matter? I wasn't doing anything wrong."

The cop held up his hand. "Slow down, pal. I wasn't accusing you of anything. Just trying to put the pieces together."

The paramedics walked past us with Jake on the board. He didn't look well at all.

"You sure look worried for a guy that doesn't know him," the cop said.

"I don't like seeing people in pain." I looked up from Jake to the cop. "I've seen enough of it to last me a lifetime."

The cop nodded. "I can understand that. I wish more people were like you." He looked over at Jake, who was now being carried through the snow. "He's probably been out here for a long time." He shook his head. "Poor bastard."

I watched as the paramedics made their way back up the path, with Jake stretched out between them.

"Which hospital are they taking him to?" I asked the cop.

"They'll take him to the clinic down on Federal Street. Hospitals won't take him. No insurance."

The paramedics loaded Jake into the back of the ambulance. A small group of people had gathered to watch. I followed the cop back through the park with enough time to watch the ambulance pull back onto the street and drive away, sirens blaring.

The clinic was on the other side of town, beside Sparky's, a computer parts store I frequented back in my motivated days. Federal Street was lined with beggars and those too sick to go anywhere else. Whenever I had to walk down Federal Street, I would keep my eyes forward the whole time and never acknowledge anyone or anything. Now that I had a reason to go there and a person to see, I couldn't help but feel like a heartless ass.

"You want a lift?" the cop asked me.

"Huh," I said, coming out of my daze. "Ah, no thanks. I'm just glad he's out of the cold." For whatever reason, I still had enough presence of mind to remember that I told the cop I didn't know him. And if I didn't know him, there would be no reason to go and see him. Nothing good ever came from lying.

The cop nodded. "Okay, then. Well, you're a good guy…" he said, pausing for my name.

"Sean."

"You may have saved his life, Sean."

The cop stepped back into his car and pulled out into traffic.

With the cop gone, I could go back to living the truth. I had to go to the clinic. I had to help Jake. I was sure that I hadn't saved anything yet.

14

I had the cabbie drop me a block from the clinic. I figured Jake was probably being examined, and I needed some time to clear my head, if that was even possible. I figured a quick walk in the brisk air might help with that. As the cab pulled away, I zipped my coat all the way up to my neck and put my hands into the pockets. I felt the pack of cigarettes Mack had given me, along with the lighter. A cigarette is exactly what I needed at that moment. I took out the pack and flipped a butt into my mouth. With the flick of my wrist, I popped the hinged top of the Zippo open and lit the butt. As I closed it, I again noticed the engraving on the side of the lighter. *Change.* It seemed like a strange word to engrave. It was typically something meaningful, like initials or a memorable date. But since Mack told me he found the lighter, I assumed the engraving meant nothing to him either. But it did make me wonder.

The clinic came into view as I rounded the corner. Surprisingly, the street was eerily empty, save for two homeless people sitting against a timeworn brick wall. They sat, curled up like bags of trash discarded by humanity with their knees up to their chests, their heads down, and dirty blankets draped over their shoulders. I had never stopped to think about their predicament in the past, about what life on the street really meant, probably because I was too preoccupied with my own problems to worry about theirs. But as I neared them, and after spending the small amount of time that I had with Jake, I realized just how difficult their lives were compared to mine.

I reached into my pocket and removed two one-hundred dollar bills, something I wasn't in a position to do before I met Mack. As I passed the two homeless men, I tapped each one on the shoulder and handed them a bill. They stared at the bill for a moment, their eyes wide. Then the homeless man on the right side stood, threw his blanket to the ground and hugged me. It was a strong embrace. He smelled awful, like a combination of piss and body odor, but that didn't matter. I put my arms around him and hugged him back. It felt so good to make a difference, even if it was a small one.

The homeless man let me go and held me out at arm's length. "Thank you," he said. He then looked back at the bill and smiled.

The second homeless man said, "I don't

think you can understand just how much this means to us." It quickly became apparent that beneath the grime, it was actually a woman. Her voice was horse, but delicate. Living on the street had taken its toll on her appearance. "Thank you," she said.

I smiled back. "You're both welcome."

I wished there was more I could do for them. I really did. But I needed to see about Jake.

As I walked a few more yards towards the clinic's door, a third homeless man approached me. I reached into my pocket for another hundred, thinking he probably saw me give his buddies some cash. I had it in my hand, but I stopped just as I was about to extend it. As the man drew closer, a mix of fear and adrenaline surged through me, propelling me to run back the way I had just come.

It was him, the sickly man, Drake, from the hallway in my apartment building. He was draped beneath a ratty black blanket.

I looked to his hands. He wasn't carrying anything. He had no gun or knife, nothing he could conceivably hurt me with. But something inside me told me he didn't need anything. He was still dressed in his morbid, black clothes. His hair blew back over his shoulders, like black tendrils of fire, trying whatever they could to escape him, but failing as miserably as I had.

I inched back on the sidewalk as he continued to slink towards me. I looked over my left shoulder, towards the homeless people I had just passed. They were gone. Not only were they gone, but everyone had seemed to disappear, leaving me alone again with the sickly man on the empty street.

"Why are you following me?" I asked, still backing up.

He said nothing. His dead eyes stared at me uncaringly.

I turned my back to him and bolted. I got no more than three steps away when I slipped on a patch of ice. I went down hard, but caught myself before my face hammered the ground. Adrenaline carried me quickly back to my feet. I spun back around.

He was gone.

I looked around nervously and searched for where he may have disappeared to. Maybe he was behind me. I turned, expecting to see his ghostly face again. Instead, the two homeless people who were not there a second ago stared at me.

I couldn't seem to catch my breath. He was

right in front of me, clear as day. I rubbed my eyes and looked around again. Still, there was no Drake to be found.

What the fuck?

I collected myself the best I could and brushed the snow off my jeans and jacket. I put my back to the wall and tried to steady my breathing. I felt as if I was about to pass out cold on the sidewalk. I didn't have time for this shit. My mental instability was going to have to wait. After a few minutes, I felt I had gathered enough of myself to see Jake. But I couldn't help but to be left feeling extremely unnerved and crazier than I'd felt in a long time.

I walked back down the sidewalk, past the place where Drake had appeared. Or, where I thought he had appeared. Real and unreal began to blend together. I then pushed open the door to the clinic. A small bell hung from the ceiling and jingled when I entered.

The clinic was busy, packed almost. It was mostly women, but there were also some children and a few men scattered about. A few heads looked up when I came in, but most didn't seem to care. This wasn't a place solely for the homeless. Anyone in need could use the clinic's services. I knew a person at Monutek that came here all the time. He said it was cheaper than paying for health insurance through the company. I hadn't even thought about health insurance up until now. I had six months left, according to Phil, but then what? What about my crazy meds? I was sure those weren't cheap. I'd have to ask Mack if this man I'd never met offered some kind of insurance plan.

As I approached the front desk, the woman behind it slid a glass divider to the side and said, "Can I help you, hon?" She was a large woman, but carried herself well. She wore no discernible makeup, aside from her bright pink eye shadow. Her braided hair was pulled back in a tight ponytail.

"I'm here to see someone."

She picked up a clipboard. "Name?"

"Sean."

She scanned her clipboard quickly. "I don't have anyone named Sean here."

I was a touch embarrassed. "I'm sorry. I thought you meant my name."

"That's okay, hon," she said with a smile.

I found it strange that she could smile surrounded by so many sick people in a free clinic. But then again, not everyone was compressed beneath the heel of depression like me. People did smile just to smile occasionally.

"Jake," I said, correcting myself. "His name is Jake."

She scanned her clipboard again. "Last name?"

"I don't know, actually."

She eyed me for a minute before looking over the sheet of names again.

"I did have a Jake here, but he left a few weeks back."

"He might not be on your list yet. He probably just got here about ten or fifteen minutes ago."

She mouthed "Oh." "Was he brought here by ambulance?"

I nodded.

"Have a seat please. I'll let the doctor know you're here."

"Thank you," I said. I turned and found one of only two open seats in the waiting room. I was stuffed in between a sleeping child, maybe two or three years old, and a woman who had her earphones turned up so loud that I found myself unintentionally humming along to "She Bop" by Cyndi Lauper.

I waited in the room for over an hour, sitting on a metal folding chair. It was hot and stuffy inside, a far cry from the outside. The smell wasn't all that great either, a mix of sick and sweat, but what could I really expect?

The amount of people in the room thinned out until only a handful were left.

I wondered what was taking so long. Were they thinking of a good way to break bad news to me? Then I began to think about how I would take bad news as it related to Jake. Would I actually be able to muster the emotions if given said news? Or would my medication block it like it normally did? I paused to think for a moment, trying to remember my past two days. I hadn't taken my meds. And surprisingly, I wasn't as emotionally unstable as I thought I should be. Sure, I had the occasional brain zaps that came with withdrawal, but not as bad as they tended to be. Then again, maybe that's why my dreams had turned to nightmares. And why I saw that Drake guy when he wasn't really there.

"Sir," the woman behind the glass said. Nobody had called me sir in a very long time, and for very good reasons. I felt old all of a sudden. "The doctor would like to speak with you." She pointed to her right. "Follow the hall all the way down to the last door on the left."

"Thanks," I said, standing. My back ached when I stood. That metal chair offered little support for my longer than expected wait.

I quickly reached the end of the short hall and knocked on the door I was told to.

The door creaked open. A sixty-something-year old Asian man stood behind it. He wore the traditional white lab coat that stopped short of his knees. A stethoscope hung around his neck. He was the dictionary picture of what a doctor should look like, with the exception of his blue shirt with a faded yellow peace symbol that peeked out from beneath the coat.

"Please," he said in almost a whisper, waving me inside.

The doctor nodded over his shoulder to an adjoining room. Jake was lying down in there. The lights above him were off, but a small nightlight shined enough for me to see that he was asleep. He had a grey blanket draped over him that rose and fell gently as he breathed.

I turned my attention back to the doctor. "Is he okay?"

"Yes and no," the doctor said. "Are you family?"

I could have said yes. Lord knows it would have made things easier. But I had lied to the cop and still felt bad about it for whatever reason. This time, I'd play it straight and let whatever was going to happen, happen.

I said, "No, not family. Just a friend."

The doctor went over to the door dividing the room we were in with Jake's. He closed it slowly, but not completely. He then waved me over to the other side of the room.

"He's in rough shape," the doctor said, looking over a chart. "I was able to stabilize him for now, but we don't have the kind of equipment here to run the tests I'd like to." The doctor paused and took a breath. "I probably shouldn't be telling you this, but with the time he has left and the fact that I doubt he has any family…"

"Is he dying?" I asked, louder and more callously than I meant to.

The doctor looked away sheepishly. He then turned back to me and nodded very softly. "I'm sorry to have to tell you that." The doctor sighed. "It's the one part of my job I truly hate." He then looked over at Jake, I assumed to make sure he was still asleep, before turning back to me. "I've taken some blood," he said. "I'll send it to the hospital for tests. But I can tell you with certainty that he has advanced symptoms of cirrhosis."

I knew of cirrhosis. I think a cousin of mine

had it. I don't know if he died or not, since I hadn't spoken to any members of my family in what seemed like forever, but I remember it being a big deal to everyone.

"Okay," I said. This must be what Mack wanted me to do. Help Jake get through this. Though how would Mack know about this? "So, what can I do to help him?"

The doctor peered through the door into Jake's room again before answering me. "Like I said, he's in the advanced stages. There's nothing you can do for him now. Just comfort him the best you can with the time he still has left."

"How much time is that exactly?"

"I'd give him a month, maybe two," the doctor said. "But realistically, he could go at any time. It depends on how long his body can hold out." The doctor shook his head. "I'm sorry." He touched my shoulder. "I've put a call in down the street at the shelter to see if they can give him a warm bed until that time comes. But they're at capacity now. I don't know how long it's going to be before a bed opens up."

"Are you sure he's dying?" I had to ask again. I knew the doctor was sure. It's what he did for a living. But I didn't want to seem to accept it.

The doctor nodded slowly, compassionately.

I knew what needed to be done. "He can come home with me," I said. "No need for him to go down the street to the shelter."

The doctor's eyes lit up. "Are you sure? His last days will be difficult on the both of you."

"I'm sure." And I really was. This is what Mack must have intended for me to do. Give him a place to stay during his final days. But how would Mack know this would happen?

The doctor gave it a quick thought. "Okay. Any place is better than the street. Let him sleep for a bit, though. He needs it." The doctor walked back towards the door that I entered through. "You can stay with him in here if you'd like. I gave him a mild sedative to help him sleep. He won't be awake for a bit."

"Thanks. I think I'll take you up on that."

The doctor nodded and left. I then sat down to think about what I had just taken on.

**

The rhythmic humming of the space heater in the room was enough of a constant to make me nod off at times while I waited for Jake to wake up. Sad thing was, the space heater threw off more heat than the clunker in my apartment. I wondered if my super would break out in a sweat in this room?

The corner of my eye caught the light in Jake's room turn on.

I rubbed the remaining sleepiness from my eyes, walked over to the door, and pushed it gently open. Jake was sitting upright on the bench. His shirt was unbuttoned half way, revealing a gnarly scar that ran down his chest, from the bottom of his neck to his bellybutton. His hair was a mess, with the left side standing up at attention. He had a mad scientist look to him.

He looked at me and furrowed his brow. "What are you doing here, kid?"

"You don't remember me finding you at the park?"

He stared at me for a moment. "That was you, huh? Don't remember much."

I nodded.

He looked at me for a minute. "You didn't do that CPR stuff on me, did you?"

"No," I said, laughing.

"Good. That's the last thing I need. Kissing some kid on the mouth." He shivered.

I laughed under my breath.

As he finished buttoning his shirt, I

fumbled with the thought of him dying. More importantly, with the fact that I had to tell him he was dying. I shouldn't have to do it. No man should have to tell another man that his life is nearing its end. But maybe this was part of what I was supposed to be doing.

"Jake, I spoke to the doctor."

Jake finished buttoning his shirt. "And what did the good doc tell you?"

I opened my mouth to speak but stopped.

"Well spit it out, kid. I ain't got all day."

"You're dying," I said, in the most abrupt and inappropriate way possible. Not at all how it should have come out of my mouth. But was there a right way to say it?

Jake was expressionless. Then he started laughing in his gurgle-filled, obstructed-throat kind of way. Certainly not what I was expecting. His laughing turned into coughing, which quickly subsided. "That must have been hard for you, kid." He hopped off the table.

"What are you laughing at?" I couldn't believe him. "Did you hear what I said? You're dying, Jake."

"Relax, kid. The doctor already told me as much." He inched closer to me. "Listen, a man knows when his time is up, and I've known for a while now. The doctor didn't tell me anything I didn't already know."

"I'm sorry," I said. It was the only thing I could think of. Maybe I should have said nothing.

"Don't be sorry," Jake said. He walked over to the table at the far wall and started to rummage through it. "I chose my own path. There's nobody to blame but myself. I came to grips with that some time ago."

I watched Jake close one drawer and then open another.

I said, "I told the doctor you'd be staying with me."

Jake didn't bother turning around, but rather kept busy in the drawer. "No thanks," he said. "I already got a place."

"You're not going back to the park, Jake. You'll only die quicker if you do."

And then it occurred to me that maybe that's what he wanted.

He pocketed something from the drawer and then closed it. He then walked back over to me and looked at me right in the eyes. "Like I said, I already got a place." He picked up his leather cap from the chair next to the door and put it back on. "But thanks, kid. I appreciate what you've done. I haven't had anyone…" He stopped himself short and looked away. "Well, anyway."

"You're staying with me. You can drop the act." Jake turned back to face me. "I'm not saying you're perfectly sane, but nobody in their right mind would choose the crap weather outside to an apartment inside." I didn't plan on giving him much of a choice. *Stubborn old bastard.* "So just cut it out, alright?"

I thought he was going to clock me again. He had that look in his eyes. How dare this *kid* talk to him that way.

He looked at me. "Alright. Looks like you got some gusto after all. Let's get going then," he said, waving me out the door as if I was the one keeping him there.

15

"You got anymore of that cheap beer?" Jake asked.

I followed him into my apartment. "Nope."

"You got anything to wet my whistle with then?"

I shook my head. "Water?"

Jake shrugged me off and sat down in front of the television.

Having no beer was fine by me. Considering the state Jake was in, and seeing how it affected Isabella, I forced myself to reevaluate my own drinking. When it came to drowning my own sorrows, the booze was a way out. But it had taken on a whole different light now. And I certainly didn't miss the pounding headache and ever-present feeling of nausea the next morning brought.

"Jake," I said. "I'll be back in a bit. I have to run an errand. Make yourself comfortable."

I walked up the flights of stairs until I once again stood in front of Isabella's door. An urge drew me to check on her. I went to knock but then froze. I heard Isabella shouting. Then I heard something break followed by a man's booming voice, closer to the door.

I knocked, instantly regretting my hasty decision. It was instinct once again. But this time, I feared it would bring a different set of results.

The shouting stopped. I heard footsteps, heavy ones, walking down Isabella's hall towards the door.

The apartment door suddenly swung open.

"What do you want?" said a giant of a man who I could only assume was her boyfriend and ex-fiancé, Sam. The sleeveless t-shirt he wore showcased his bulging and overly hairy arms. His broad shoulders spanned the entirety of the doorway. He was larger than I had envisioned, and that wasn't good.

"Sean," Isabella said from the other end of the hall.

Sam turned back. "You know this guy?"

Isabella ran up the hall, but Sam blocked the door. "Get out of my way, Sam." She squirmed her way beneath his arm and out into the hall. "Now's not a good time, Sean."

"Is everything alright?" I asked.

I didn't dare look, but I could feel Sam's branding stare on me. I hadn't felt this way since high school, not since I'd been bullied into almost dropping out. I felt very clammy all of a sudden. I pushed it aside. Now wasn't about me. I needed to help Isabella.

Isabella went to answer me, but Sam interjected. "Everything's fine," he said, moving his attention from me to Isabella. "Come back inside, Bella."

I don't know where it came from, but I said, "I asked Isabella if everything was alright." The last part came out squeaky, mousy. The tough guy act wasn't mine to do. I was out of place even saying the words, let alone trying to hold up the act.

That pissed Sam off. He flared his nostrils and scrunched his brow. I thought for sure cartoon smoke was going to shoot out of his nose and ears. He took his hand off the doorjamb and took a step into the hall and closer to me. I could have sworn the floor rumbled as he walked.

"Sam," Isabella said. She sounded alarmed. "Leave him alone."

I stood my ground, all the while remembering what it was like to be bullied, thinking about all the laughing at my expense, drowning in the memories of my most helpless moments. I felt more helpless now than I did then. I was more out of my league. At least in high school, there was always that lingering teacher to stop it. The most I'd get is an atomic wedgie, possibly some bruises, but the mental anguish was the one part that never truly faded. The endless mental torture I'd put myself through, wondering if what the bullies said was true, looking for self-worth despite their barbed words. I wouldn't let that happen again. Not to me. Not to anyone.

Sam said, "You messing around with my girl?" His words wafted with the smell of beer.

"It's nothing like that," Isabella said, stepping to the side of us.

Sam turned to her. "Stay out of this, Bella. Get back inside."

Isabella stared right at him, angry. She took a step back but remained in the hall.

He turned back to me. "You have a little crush on my girl, do you?"

"It's not like that," I said. "We're just friends."

"Friends, huh? Sure looks like more than that from where I'm standing."

Isabella said, "Sam, please."

He turned to her again. "Didn't I tell you to get back inside?" He nodded to the open apartment door. "Now go."

Isabella took another step towards the

door, almost with one foot inside. She looked at me. I could tell she was scared, an emotion we shared at that moment. Seeing her like that conjured up hateful, angry emotions. I couldn't remember ever feeling so strongly about something as I did at that moment.

Sam turned back to me again. He leaned in and looked down. "This is your one chance," he said. "Leave and go back to wherever you came from." He paused. "And don't let me ever see you here again. Got me?"

I turned my attention away from him and over to Isabella. "Come with me," I said.

Isabella hesitantly took a step towards me.

Sam swung his left arm out and blocked her.

She pushed his arm away like an ant attempting to lift a tree. "Let me go, Sam. What are you trying to do?"

"I said, get back inside." Sam then grabbed her by the arms and held her.

She spit in his face and he retaliated by backhanding her across hers.

Isabella crumbled to the floor of the hallway.

When he turned back to me, I threw the hardest punch I'd ever thrown, a right hook that hit him squarely in the jaw. It was like punching the side of a building. My hand throbbed at the knuckles. I didn't even know where it came from. I don't remember thinking about punching him, or actually moving my arm. I just remembered the contact my fist made and then the look of complete shock on Sam's face.

Sam then returned the punch, knocking me across the hall and into the wall. I slid down onto the floor. My world spun around me. I felt exactly how I did after too many drinks. I was out of it, but not enough to forget what got me there.

"Sam!" Isabella screamed. She was back on her feet and started to pound on his back. "Stop it!"

Sam spun around and delivered another backhand, knocking her out cold. Blood seeped from a small gash on her forehead. He then lumbered over to me, picked me up off the floor, and tossed me back across the hall.

I flew through the open apartment door and rolled partway down Isabella's hall, finally stopping at the legs of a nearby table. I tried to shake it off, but the dizziness remained.

I looked back in time to see Sam drag Isabella back into the apartment and shut the door. He didn't bother checking on her. I assumed he just didn't want anyone to come snooping.

"I gave you your chance, buddy," he said, walking towards me. "I was being a nice guy. Then you had to go and hit me. And I don't much like being hit."

I got back up on my wobbly feet and left the close quarters of the hall for the living room.

As soon as I ran out of space, I turned back around. Then, gushing with too many feelings to sort out, I ran full speed at Sam with my shoulder down. I hit him, but he barely budged, like a flea on a dog. He then threw me across the room as if gravity had expired. I knocked over the picture-filled mantle and bounced off the couch, landing next to the coffee table.

Before I could react, he grabbed the back of my shirt and pulled me off the ground. I literally saw stars when he clocked me on the right side of my face. I fell back down, bleeding from my lip.

"Maybe this will teach you to mind your own business," Sam said, picking me up off the floor again.

He turned me around to face him. My dizziness made it look like there was two of him, zigzagging back and forth between each other. My eyelids were heavy. Sam sneered at me and then threw me onto the couch.

He then walked away and back up the hall towards Isabella.

Anger subdued my pain. It pushed me off the couch and onto my wobbly feet. My blood boiled. At that moment I didn't care what happened to me. I tried to commit suicide a few days ago, what was he going to do to me that I hadn't already tried?

I reached down and grabbed a heavy brass table lamp that had fallen in the scuffle. It clinked as I picked it up.

Sam must have heard it. He turned back to me and raced down the hall like a charging bull.

I held the lamp to my right side by its neck, the base of it free to be swung.

Sam neared. I held fast and gripped the lamp tight.

I swung.

He ducked.

The charging bull hit me with the force of a bullet and carried me across the room and into the kitchen table. I slid across the top and onto the floor. The table fell on top of me. The chairs scattered.

"Gotta be a hero, huh?" he said, tossing the table to the side. "Tough guy with the lamp." He palmed for me beneath the remaining chairs.

My bones felt broken, all of them. I didn't think they were. But it felt that way.

I looked to my right. A broken chair leg. Without thinking, I gripped it and swung with everything I had left. Again, it was instinct driving me. But this time, it proved well-timed. The chair leg connected with the right side of Sam's face. He fell back off his feet and hard onto his butt. I stood, pushed up by a surge of adrenaline and the need to finish this before he finished me.

I walked over to him. The right side of his face was covered in blood from where the chair leg had connected.

"It takes a tough man to beat up a woman," I said. I had no idea where it was all coming from. Even though I was in considerable pain, I felt alive.

I swung the chair leg again, this time with both hands. It hit his arm as he covered his face. And though the leg vibrated in my hand as if it hit steel, the look on his face told me he felt every bit of the impact.

"Listen, buddy," he said. "This is just a big

misunderstanding." His words were slurred and unimportant to me at that point.

I couldn't believe this giant of a man was actually trying to reason me out of hitting him again. I was in a position of power I had never been in. And it felt great.

I swung again, hitting the same arm.

"You've probably done this your whole life," I said. "Torment the easy targets, people you'd never have to worry about fighting back. I wouldn't be surprised if you got off thinking about it." I whacked him in the arm again, harder than before. He went to stand, but I inched closer to him with the chair leg above my head.

He conceded and put the arm I hadn't hit in the air between us.

But I wasn't done talking. I was like an erupting volcano, dormant for too many years. I had too many feelings that needed to be felt.

I quickly looked away, only for a second so he couldn't take advantage of it. Isabella was still out cold in the middle of the hall.

I turned back. "Does it make you feel good hitting her like that? Smacking around someone half your size? All because she had a change of heart before your marriage?"

"Screw you," he said, trying to grab me.

I hit him again. This time on his temple. His head slumped to his left shoulder.

I looked over at Isabella again. She wasn't stirring. I worried for her, especially since she was only feet away and I hadn't checked on her yet, but I couldn't go to her until I was sure she was safe.

I went to my knees. I then reached for Sam's bloodied neck to make certain he was still alive. I couldn't be sure. I didn't pull even one of my swings. And I had no remorse over that.

A steady thump pulsed beneath my fingers. He was alive. Part of me was glad that I hadn't killed him, but the other part of me, the one riding on a wave of emotions, wasn't so happy.

I then turned to go check on Isabella.

"I beat her like I beat your mother," Sam said from behind me.

What?

I looked back at him, his face still turned to the side. "What did you say?"

Sam laughed in a sinister way. "That damn whore never did anything right."

My throat closed up a bit. Unbridled rage surged through me.

"How dare you call my mother a whore.

She was a saint. A saint!" I screamed. "She was one of the only good people on this horrid planet. But instead of her, I'm surrounded by people like you." I was so consumed by rage at the time that I hadn't stopped to think of how he even knew my mother. My only consideration at that point was to defend her.

When he turned his head to look at me, I literally fell back, horrified by what I saw. The blood-covered face was no longer that of Sam's, but of my Father's. My ears rang. My head pounded and numbed at the same time.

"Your mother left you because she hated you," Sam said. "She couldn't wait to be free of you."

I was going crazy. No, not going, I had gone crazy. My Father was dead, thankfully scrubbed from the Earth some time back. Everyone was better off for it. Yet there he was, feet away from me, tormenting me as if he never left. I wanted to move but I was frozen in place.

"She died from cancer," I said, refuting the argument of a dead person. "She had no choice but to leave."

He smiled. "She was fine until you were born. That's when she got sick. You made her sick, you selfish bastard. You're the one that killed her."

"Shut up," I barked. "Shut your damn mouth."

My Mother's diagnosis did reveal she probably got cancer around the time I was born. But the doctors told her that the two were in no way related. At least, that's what I heard her telling someone on the phone one day. My Father had alluded in a roundabout way after she passed that I had something to do with it. But nothing like this. Whatever *this* was.

He started to laugh again. Blood dripped from the side of his head. "You killed her," he said again. "You're to blame."

"No," I said, shaking my head. I wouldn't allow the monster to play with me from beyond the grave. "She didn't die because of me. She loved me. She protected me." I looked at him. "She hated you. I hated you." More rage built inside me. I wanted to leap across the room and rip his head off.

He spit more blood and wiped his mouth. He just stared at me with his lifeless eyes; eyes I had thankfully not seen in years.

I broke the invisible bond holding me down and stood. "It wasn't my fault she died. If anything, it was you pushing her closer to the brink every day. I was only a kid at the time. How was I supposed to know anything then?" I felt tears fall down my cheeks. "You beat her and when you were done with her, you came after me, your only child, and you beat me without remorse. I fucking hate you. I'm glad you're dead."

"You deserved it," he said.

I ran over to him, dropped to my knees, and grabbed him by the shirt with both hands. I pulled him in closer.

"No," I said. "I didn't deserve it. She didn't deserve it. Nobody deserves what you did. Nobody. You were a terrible, terrible man. You ruined both of our lives. And when Mom died…" I had to stop and collect myself. Not the tears, as they didn't matter to me, but I became too chocked up to continue.

Thinking of my Mother, beaten and bloody, cancer-stricken and crying, just made me sad in the deepest parts of my heart. That was no way to live. She was so sweet and innocent, such an amazing person. Why was it that the best people were always tested with the worst situations?

"When Mom died," I said louder than I had intended, "it was just the two of us left. And rather than step up and be the man you should have been, you beat me more and made me feel guilty for what happened." I pushed him back against the wall and wiped the tears from my eyes. "I was a kid, Dad." I hated even referring to him as Dad. "I didn't know anything except the love of my dead Mother and the hate of my living Father. I hate you now as much as I hated you then. I'd give my life to bring Mom back."

I looked at him. I was tired and out of breath. But I was also seeing clearly for the first time in a long time. "It wasn't my fault. None of it was. I'm through blaming myself for what you did. You're the monster, not me." I stood and dropped the wooden leg. "And you can rot in hell for all I care."

I left him slumped against the wall and went to check on Isabella.

She was stirring now, holding her head with her left hand.

I bent down and put my hand on her back. "Are you okay?" The gash on her head looked superficial, thankfully.

She nodded slowly. "I think so." She looked up at me. "Where is he?"

I looked back down the hall towards his legs, which were motionless.

Isabella said, "Did you do that?"

I nodded. A strange feeling of satisfaction dwelled within me at that moment. Never in a million years would I have thought it possible, but boy was I glad I did. It felt immensely liberating.

I helped Isabella to her feet and steadied her while she regained her balance. I then reached up and wiped a bit of the blood off her head. “I think you’ll be okay. Doesn’t look like it needs stitches.”

She rotated her right arm in a circle and winced. “I can tell you this much, that is the last time he puts his hands on me.”

I was happy to hear that. But now that her safety was out of my mind, my Father’s face popped back in, unwanted like when he was still alive. I walked back down the hall and rounded the corner. When I looked down, it was no longer the monster I once knew as my Father, but Sam again. A very bloody and groggy Sam.

I righted one of the fallen chairs and sat down. I stared at Sam as he lay there, picturing my Father’s face tormenting me. With only a second to think about what had happened, I couldn’t help but to feel a small sense of relief. I hurt from being thrown around, and my mind certainly wasn’t right, possibly schizophrenic for seeing what I had, but the world seemed a bit brighter despite it all. And I felt as if I had helped Isabella the way that Mack had intended. I protected her when she needed it.

16

The police stormed into Isabella's apartment with their guns drawn.

"Hold it right there," one of the officers shouted.

Both Isabella and I looked to the doorway in shock. They were a bit late to the party.

Behind the incoming officers, standing in the hall, was a short old lady with curlers still in her white hair. She stood on her tiptoes and tried to look over the officers' shoulders through her thick, black-rimmed glasses.

"That's him," she said. She pointed to me. Or near me, anyway.

The officer in the back looked over his shoulder. "You sure, ma'am?"

I stared at her as she stared at me. I knew right then that only one of us could actually see the other.

She nodded, though what appeared to be reluctantly.

"Officers," Isabella said. "There's been a mistake." She pointed down at Sam. "That's the man you want to arrest. Not Sean."

The officer looked down at Sam and then back at me. It was apparent to me he was trying to figure out how I, this scrap of a man, beat up the giant on the floor. I still hadn't figured that part out myself. Not only had I beat him up, but I destroyed the right side of his face to a point where there was more blood than flesh showing. Not my intent, but I was forced into a situation I didn't want any part of. I felt like I had been fighting for my life. And in a strange, hard-to-explain kind of way, I felt like I was fighting for my mother.

The officer then bent down and gauged the severity of Sam's wounds. He held two fingers to his wrist. The cop then leaned into his shoulder walkie-talkie and pushed the button. "Unit 213."

The dispatcher chimed back, "Copy Unit 213, what's your status?"

"We're going to need paramedics onsite for a male, late thirties, lacerations to the face with heavy bleeding. Victim has a pulse but is unconscious." He then stood up and faced me. "Sir, please stand and put your hands behind your back."

"You're making a mistake," I said, standing. "I was just defending myself." I wasn't expecting this for sure. "He was beating her."

The cop turned me around and cuffed me.

He said, "We'll get this all sorted out down at the station. You're not under arrest at the moment. But we'll need to detain you until we get all the facts sorted out."

"Officer," Isabella said. "He was protecting me."

"That may be the case, ma'am. But I have one man bleeding and unconscious on the ground. I can't very well get his side of the story now. And we have a witness saying that's not how it happened." He looked over his shoulder into the hall.

Isabella looked to the hall as well. She turned back to the officer and said, "You mean to tell me you're taking the word of Mrs. Janis over ours?" She laughed. "She might as well be legally blind." She then nodded towards Mrs. Janis in the hall, who still looked on through her thick spectacles. "Thanks Mrs. Janis. You're a real big help."

Mrs. Janis smiled politely and waved.

I turned to Isabella. "It's alright. I'm sure this will all get sorted out." I smiled at her to hide my lie. I wasn't sure if this would get sorted out. Obviously, Sam wasn't going to just come clean and tell it like it was. He was a vindictive drunk from what I'd seen and heard. Not the best person to have to rely on for a truthful retelling of an event such as this.

"I'm so sorry, Sean," Isabella said. "This is all because of me."

"Don't be." I wanted to hug her, reassure her that I was fine, but my newly cuffed hands prohibited that. "I did what needed to be done. None of this is your fault, Isabella. You can't take the blame for someone else's actions. My mother lived a tormented life because of my abusive father. If you escape that same fate, then all of this will be well worth it."

She smiled and gave me a kiss on my cheek. She then turned to the cop who had cuffed me. "Where are you taking him?"

"First precinct, ma'am." He nodded down the hall to his partner. "Officer Roy will take your statement."

"Can't I go with Sean?" she asked.

The officer shook his head. "No ma'am." He offered no more.

The feelings of satisfaction I had from my encounter with Sam had vanished. Now the present situation took over. I was cuffed and being escorted out of Isabella's apartment for doing the right thing. Even though the officer said I wasn't under arrest, it sure felt like it. He took no leniency when handling me. The cuffs dug into my wrists.

"I'll be down to get you as quickly as I can," Isabella said.

I smiled back and nodded.

The hall was much more crowded as the officer guided me out of the apartment. Lots of neighbors now. Where were they when I needed some help? It would have been nice if someone with some semblance of good vision had been around during the confrontation. Instead, I was ratted out by Mrs. Magoo and her soda bottle glasses.

The officer stuffed me into the back of the cruiser. My knees were jammed tight against the front bench seat. A piece of thick plastic separated me from the arresting officer. Something inside me wanted me to converse with the cop, tell him how innocent I was, that I was just doing a good deed to help out a woman in need. He'd have to see it my way. But I kept to myself instead. I felt like I would be wasting my breath trying to turn him around. If the law was innocent until proven guilty, then I didn't even have a need to explain myself. However, that's not how the justice system worked in my eyes. I knew I was screwed unless the odds became tipped in my favor, something I wasn't counting on.

We arrived at the police station and went

into the underground parking lot. We pulled up to a grey metal door with a single, wire mesh window in it. The cop unloaded me from the back of the cruiser with a bit more care than before and walked me up to the door. He looked up to the camera above the door. A quick buzz and the door unlocked.

He walked me past a thick glass window with two ladies sitting behind it. They had a row of computer monitors in front of them and the word "Dispatch" painted on the wall behind them.

Another buzz and a second door opened.

The officer walked me past a row of desks and up to a man sitting beside a large cell. There was only two other people inside. Each sat on opposite sides of the cell with their heads down. Neither paid a lick of attention to me.

"What do you got, Harry?" the officer beside the cell said.

The arresting officer stopped us. "Just detaining him. One of the parties involved was unconscious when we got there. We'll need his statement to get this sorted out."

The officer nodded and went to the far wall. He pulled up a plastic case and hit the button beneath it. Another buzz followed by a loud click. He then walked back the short distance and pulled open the holding cell's door.

The officer holding me unlocked the cuffs. "This is just until we get things sorted out. Like I said before, you're not under arrest. Just standard procedure."

I nodded. I wasn't happy about the situation, but it was beyond my control. It's not like I was going to suddenly flee the police station. I walked into the holding cell. The door quickly shut behind me. One of the two others in the cell looked up at me. His right eye was swollen. As quickly as he looked up, he looked back down. The other man stayed in the corner's shadow, with his knees tucked into his chest and his head buried.

I sat down closest to the door on a beat-up metal bench and sighed. What had I gotten myself into? All the money in the world wasn't worth this crap. But the look on Isabella's face was. But for all I knew, I was hours away from getting booked for battery, or worse. Then my mind started racing. I hit Sam with the leg of the chair. Could that be considered a deadly weapon? I was pretty sure that kicking someone while they're down was considered assault with a deadly weapon. And if a human leg was a deadly weapon, then the carved wooden chair leg sure as hell was.

An officer walked to the cell door. "Brooks," he said, looking at the man to my right, the one with the swollen eye that looked up at me briefly. "Come with me."

The cell door again buzzed open. The haggard man rose to his feet and sulked his way over to the officer, zigzagging, drunk. The door closed as quickly as it opened, leaving me alone with the only other person in there.

I stood and walked over to the area where Brooks just was. It put more distance between me and the other guy. The cell was large, no need to be on top of each other.

I sat down and leaned against the back wall.

It was at that moment that it all hit me. A few days ago, I was sitting in my cubicle at Monutek, dazing the days away, and now I was in a holding tank at the police station for sticking up for a woman I had just met. Life sure had a way of fucking with me. I had gone from one confining cell to another. I wasn't the type to get involved. I'd rather sit in the shadows and be hidden from responsibility. But there I was.

"What are you here for?" said the man to

my right in a whisper. His voice sounded familiar.

I looked over. He still had his head buried. I could barely hear him over the bustle of the police station.

"What?" I asked. I wasn't in the mood for this right now.

The man nodded to the officers outside the doors, but kept his head down. "What did they get you for?"

"It's just a mistake," I said. "I should be out of here soon." I was lying to myself. Maybe it was to keep me from wanting to kill myself again. I tucked my knees up on the bench and stared down at them. Sam's bloodied face stuck in my mind. What if he died because of what I did? I'd be a murderer. And what was I going to tell them? That my dead father's face replaced Sam's and that's why it became worse than it should have?

The man laughed. "You shouldn't have helped her." He raised his voice from a whisper. "Look what it brought you."

A chill ran down my spine. That voice was imprinted on my mind, branded by the hottest of irons. The hairs on the back of my neck again stood tall.

I told myself there was no way it was him.

For the sickly man, Drake, to be in the same holding cell that I was, at the same time, on the same day was a near impossibility. Forcing myself to look over, however, quickly made the impossible possible.

Drake said, "I tried to warn you, Sean." He stood and casually walked over to my bench. He dragged his gimpy leg behind him. "You did not heed my words, friend."

"We're not friends," I said. Though I'm sure he knew that already. "Officers!" I yelled. I looked outside the bars to find the police station empty, just as the street was outside the clinic.

Drake sat down in front of me on the bench. It was like sitting across from a corpse. He had this dark and omnipotent power over me. I wanted to get up and run to the cell door, but something held me firmly in place, as it had during our first encounter. I had to listen, but not because I wanted to.

Drake licked his lower lip and said, "You have to stop before it gets to a point where you cannot. I would hate to see that happen. For your own well-being."

I found the power to speak. "I know who you are, Drake."

He smiled as if he relished in the fact that I

knew something about him.

"Go on," he said.

"Mack told me about you, about how you used to work with him."

Drake smiled, revealing his rotting teeth. "Is that what he told you? That we worked together?"

I nodded. "You two have your differences. That's between you and him. I don't want anything to do with it."

"But you have everything to do with it, Sean." He said my name in an exaggerated manner, drawing it out in the middle. "The very thing that got you in this cell is also the very thing that binds you and me."

"What are you talking about?"

"It's quite simple, Sean. When you help him, you hurt me. And when you hurt me, I get very angry."

Where the hell did everyone go?

"Help," I yelled.

I turned back. Drake was right there, standing before me. His ghostly face inches from mine.

"Why are you doing this?" I asked.

"I'm not doing anything, Sean." He backed up a bit and casually walked to the other side of the cell. "You are the one to blame."

I pointed at myself instinctively. "Me? How am I doing this?"

He backed me against the cage. Despite his gimpy leg, he seemed to hover at times, moving faster than comprehension. I looked deep into his dead eyes.

He tilted his head a bit and said, "I warned you once. But you did not listen to me. So I am telling you again. Don't help the bald man. He's trying to change you." He backed away. He held his hands out to the sides. "If you do, it will come with severe consequences. This is the final warning you will get."

Everything went completely dark. I couldn't see a thing.

When the lights flickered back on a moment later, the cell was empty.

I turned. The steady flow of officers were back now as if they'd been there the whole time.

I ran to the cell door. "Where were you?"

The officer outside the cell looked at me funny. He looked around at everyone else and then back at me. "I've been sitting here watching you talk to yourself, fella."

"So you saw him?" I asked.

"Saw who?"

"The other guy in the cell with me. Drake."

The cop looked at me cockeyed. "Buddy, you on drugs or something? There were only two of you in there and the other guy just got released. He walked right by you."

"No, there were three of us," I said. "I'm sure of it."

The cop stood up and walked over to the cell door. He stood face to face with me, with only the thick cell bars separating us.

"Listen, pal," he said. "I think I know how many guys I have in the holding tank. You're the only one left."

I turned and scanned the cell frantically. I was the only one in the tank. But what did that mean? What the hell was going on with me?

I started to breath heavily again. I didn't feel right at all. Panic attack. *Slow, controlled breaths. Come on, Sean. Pull it together.*

The officer backed off his hardline stance. "You don't look so hot, pal," he said. "You feeling alright?"

I thought I was doing the right thing by helping out Isabella, and in turn doing my job for Mack. I mean, it felt good to help her. Real good. So how was I hurting Drake by doing it? Why did he have such a hatred for Mack? Why was I so stupid to get involved in all of this in the first place? Life would have been so much easier if I was dead.

A man walked up from behind the officer and up to the bars. He wore a white button-down shirt with the sleeves rolled up and a green and black tie.

"Mr. O'Rourke," he said. "I'm Detective Fin. Come with me, please." He nodded for the officer to open the door.

I followed the man through the back of the police station and into a room filled with desks buried beneath waves of paper. We stopped at one of the desks in the center of the room.

He sat down and nodded for me to do the same. He then picked up a paper, looked it over quickly, then put it down on his desk with the array of others.

"Mr. Thomas is awake," Fin said.

At first I thought he had the wrong person. Who was Mr. Thomas? He must have seen the quick burst of confusion in my eyes.

"The guy you beat up?" he said.

I mouthed "Oh," unsure of what else to say. I still couldn't get Drake's morbid face out of my head. I hoped I didn't look as crazy as I felt.

"Nineteen stitches across his head. That's what it took to stop the bleeding." He looked at me as if I should be apologizing to him for what I did.

I had no intention of apologizing to anyone. I was done blaming myself for every little thing that I had nothing to do with. I did nothing wrong. People should be patting me on the back for what I did. I felt as if I should have said something. However, I felt guilty with the way he stared at me, like he was probing me for information without asking the questions. I'd watched a lot of cop shows and couldn't help but to feel like I knew the techniques, even though most were nothing more than devices put in to make the show better.

"You can relax, Mr. O'Rourke. We know you're innocent."

A huge weight felt like it was instantly lifted off my shoulders.

Detective Fin said, "The story you told the arresting officer matches Ms. Santino's story."

So that's Isabella's last name.

The detective continued. "And we had some of the neighbors questioned and it turns out this isn't the first incident. Apparently, Mr. Thomas has quite the temper. Arrested once for battery a couple of years ago while on vacation down south. He put that guy in the emergency room. Be happy your circumstances were different." He flipped through a couple pieces of paper and looked back at me. "As soon as he's well enough, he'll stand trial. Most likely facing some jail time."

It was such a relief to hear those words. "So," I said. "I'm free to go?"

Detective Fin nodded. "We'll need to get your official statement of what happened, but after that you're free to go. We may contact you with some follow-up questions, but most likely this will be the end of it."

"Thanks," I said.

"No, Mr. O'Rourke. Thank you for being a stand-up guy. I see a lot of abuse, and too few people actually do something about it. Most turn a blind eye because it's not their problem. You may have saved her life by making it your problem."

I said, "I don't think it was that bad."

"Maybe not when you got there. But who's to say what would have happened if you hadn't been there?" He let the words hang in the air for a moment. "He's an alcoholic with a bad temper and a record. Trust me when I tell you, you saved her life in more than one way. I've had far too many of these turn-up the other way. I wish there were more people like you. I truly do." He leaned back in his chair. "It sure as hell would make my job a little easier."

"Is Isabella okay?"

He nodded. "She's fine. The paramedics checked her out before removing Mr. Thomas from the apartment. A couple of cuts and bruises, but nothing she won't recover from." He leaned his chair forward, sitting upright, and pulled in closer to the desk. "Larry," he shouted over the noise. A uniformed officer walked over. "Can you take Mr. O'Rourke's statement for me?"

Larry nodded.

I stood and followed Larry to give my statement.

When I was done retelling what had happened, Larry escorted me from the back of the station and into the busier front.

"Sean," Isabella said, running up and throwing her arms around me. "Thank you." She buried her head in my chest and hugged me with the strength of a bear. My bruised ribs throbbed in pain, but her embrace felt good. Despite being in the middle of a crowded police station, I closed my eyes and lived in the moment.

"You don't need to thank me, Isabella."

She let me go but stayed within arm's reach. "No. That's exactly what I need to do.

It's what I want to do. If you hadn't knocked on my door the other day from out of the blue, I would have probably been in my apartment right now, bleeding," she paused, "or worse. You saved me from Sam and from my own life. And that's something I couldn't have done on my own."

I did help her. And it felt damn good. I only wished I could have done the same for my mother. But, in a roundabout way, maybe I had.

17

"Long errand," Jake said, looking at me over his shoulder.

I had forgotten Jake was even there. With everything that had happened, he was the last thing on my mind. I looked at him, but didn't say anything. I didn't have the energy to explain what I'd just been through.

He got up, brushed some crumbs off his shirt, and said, "I figured I'd go to the store and pick up some essentials while you were out. You know, you shouldn't leave piles of money laying around like that."

"That's fine," I said. I'd forgotten about the money, too. None of it really mattered at the moment.

"Oh, and someone slid this under the door for you." He handed me an envelope, the same kind that started all this, green and shiny.

I took the envelope and put it in the back pocket of my jeans. An envelope just like that one got me into a fight and thrown in jail. Not to mention starting me down a road I didn't think would wind like it had.

Jake walked over to the fridge and pulled

out two beers. He walked them over to me and held out the one in his right hand. "I picked up some beer," he said. "You were all out."

A beer would have tasted great at that moment. And it certainly would have put me in better spirits. But after seeing firsthand what the alcohol did to Isabella's life, I just couldn't bring myself to even take a sip of it. I didn't want to turn out like Sam. And while I didn't have the temperament for violence, jail may have been my best-case scenario.

"No thanks," I said. I walked past Jake and flopped down on my couch. I would have loved to draw the blinds and sleep for days.

Jake shrugged and sat back in the chair, not bothering to put the second beer in the fridge. He cracked one of them and took a long gulp before turning the chair around to face me. "You okay?" he asked.

"I'll be fine."

"You sure about that? Not for nothing, but you look like shit."

I nodded very softly. I wasn't sure of anything anymore. A sudden pang of anger shot through me. I sat up on the couch and banged on the wall as hard as I could.

"Harry," I shouted. "Turn down your damn TV." I banged again. It was the last thing

I wanted to deal with right then.

I don't know what came over me, but I needed to get out the aggression that had been building for too long. I banged again. The TV volume stayed as it was, loud and annoying. I stomped across my living room like a child throwing a temper tantrum and out my front door. I headed left and stopped a few feet later at Harry's front door.

I knocked, loudly. "Harry," I said. "It's Sean. Open up."

I waited. The anger inside me brewed to the top like a shaken soda bottle ready to explode.

I knocked again. Nothing. I figured he couldn't hear me over that damn noise of his. *He probably turned off his hearing aid again*. I didn't think, I just reacted and reached for the door knob. I quickly turned it and was surprised to find it unlocked. The door creaked open.

I pushed the door open a bit more. "Harry, you home?" I shouted. It was definitely loud enough to hear as my throat hurt. He didn't answer.

I looked around the empty hallway before creeping into Harry's apartment. It was extremely dark in there, darker than I had my own apartment, and I loved the dark. It also smelled funny. Not a weird kind of scent, but more of a stagnant, swampy kind of odor.

The TV's volume was so much louder in his apartment than it was in mine.

I looked into the far right corner, past the windows that were covered up with dark blue sheets. The top of Harry's head poked up over his chair. The TV was tuned into some kind of infomercial, as usual. The guy loved his useless items.

"Harry," I said. "Didn't you hear me banging?" I knew he couldn't hear me, but I did want to announce myself, especially since I came in uninvited. The last thing I wanted was to go shocking him into a heart attack or something.

It was too late for that, though.

Harry's mouth was agape, his eyes wide open, and he was staring at the ceiling. I was no doctor, but it was clear that Harry couldn't hear me because he was dead. He must have died a while back, because the strong, swampy smell was strongest next to him.

It was creepy being in there, alone in the dark with a dead guy. But not as creepy as the first time this happened to me. I was seven or eight years old when I had been accidentally locked in the funeral parlor with my aunt's corpse. I slipped away during the wake to take a nap. Looking at dead people wasn't really my thing. And it was so quiet in that closet. Then my nap turned into something longer. Once everyone left, it became far too quiet. I freaked out a bit. All the doors were locked, except for the room where my aunt was. I came to find out that my parents thought my grandparents had taken me home. I spent a solid three or four hours in there before my mom came and found me. We went for ice cream after that. Typical parenting fallback that worked to smooth over almost any situation. The ice cream tasted good, but not good enough to make me forget the bad postmortem make-up job on my aunt, one cheek rosier than the other.

"He doesn't look so good," Jake said, standing no more than a foot behind me.

"Damn it, Jake," I said. "You scared the crap out of me."

He took a sip of his beer. "I've seen a lot like him, out on the streets." Jake walked past me and stood between the TV and a very dead Harry. "Yup," he said, looking at Harry and then back to me. "He's definitely dead." He then walked to Harry and leaned in closer to him, almost to a point where it was creepy. He stared at his eyes. "When you look into a man's eyes and nothing looks back, it's a sure sign." He then stood back up and looked over at me.

I felt bad for banging on the wall now. I felt even worse for the misplaced anger I had felt towards a dead man. I turned off the TV and picked up Harry's phone, which was buried beneath a small stack of yellowing newspapers.

"911, what's your emergency?"

"My neighbor's dead," is what I blurted out. I didn't have the energy to dance around the facts.

I gave the operator our location and told her I would stay until the paramedics arrived. I then sat on the couch against the windows and stared across at Harry. Jake sat next to me.

Jake held out his bottle of beer and pointed it towards Harry. "I used to have a chair like that." He took a swig of his beer. "Except mine was black leather. Comfortable as hell."

"Where's the chair now?" I said.

Jake looked over at me and then down to his lap. I expected no response, but then surprisingly Jake said, "Don't know where it is now. My guess is its right where I left it."

"And where would that be, Jake?"

Jake finished his beer, put the empty one down on the floor between his feet, and cracked the new one. He looked over his shoulder at me. "I wasn't always homeless you know, kid. I used to have a life." He paused in what looked to be a moment of self-reflection. "A pretty damn good life, too."

"So what happened?" This was it. Finally, Jake's shell appeared to be cracking.

"I made some bad choices. That's what happened."

"What kind of choices?"

Jake leaned back on the couch and rested the beer on his mound of a stomach. "You ever make bad decisions, kid?" He looked over to me.

I almost laughed right then and there. "My whole life is a never-ending bad decision."

"Well," he said. "I know how that goes."

I joined him in looking at Harry. I can say this, though. If I had died, the last thing I would want would be two people staring at me, talking about their woes. But that's what happened.

"What happened?" I asked Jake. I expected him to tighten up like last time and shoot me a look. But he didn't. I didn't know if it was the beer talking or if Jake was just getting used to me, but the barrier between us seemed thinner than before.

"My life used to be everything I ever wanted and then some." He suddenly stood from the couch and walked over to the window. He drew the blue sheet to the right. Light flooded into the apartment and made Harry look so much paler and, well, deader. "But then I threw it all away because I had no control over myself." He then tipped his beer back and finished it.

"So where did that life go? Why are you living in the park when you have that life waiting for you?"

"There's nothing waiting for me, kid. Truth is, you can only be selfish for so long. After a while, life moves on without you." Jake looked back at me and I could have sworn he had watery eyes when he did. But he quickly looked back out the window. "I had a high paying job, a nice house in the suburbs, a beautiful wife, an amazing daughter."

"So what happened to it all?"

"I threw it all away, kid. Over problems that I couldn't control. I lost it all with one too many throws of the dice. And then I buried those memories in booze."

"Gambling?"

Jake nodded.

My stomach knotted up. I knew all too well what gambling brought. Sure, there were the lucky few who made a living out of it. But their living came at the expense of thousands of others who thought they were good enough to be one of the elite. I was one of those thousands of unlucky people living the delusion.

"I'm sorry," I said. "I can relate."

He looked at me to continue.

I didn't want to relive it, but I felt as if I should since Jake opened up to me. "I was engaged about six years ago. Her name was Beth, and she was amazing in every way." I stopped talking for a moment and looked down. I tried to keep any and every thought of Beth out of my mind. It was just too painful to remember how badly I messed up. But now the memories were there for me to retell. "She told me I had a problem. But I didn't listen. Not until it was too late. I went to the casino one night and came home to a dark house and a short note with the engagement ring I gave her on top of it."

That was the last I saw of her. She changed her email address and phone number. And that was enough to end my search. I could have done more. Booze does a funny thing to a man's motivation, however.

I continued. "Thing is, even after she left me, I didn't stop. I ended up selling her ring at some sleazy pawn shop one night in a drunken stupor and lost that money on one spin of the roulette wheel. One fucking spin. I knew I should have picked red. I ran out of money after that. From then on, I promised myself never to gamble again. It's the one and only promise I've actually kept over the years."

I hadn't kept the promise because I was strong. I wasn't strong in any sense. I couldn't fool myself into believing that. The promise remained intact because I just didn't have the motivation to gamble anymore. The high I got from the occasional win wasn't enough to battle the utter despair I felt when I lost. And I needed my money for more important things, like beer.

"So why do you seem so unhappy?" Jake said. "You beat your gambling problem, right? That's better than most people can do. You're always moping around. Are you ever happy, kid?"

I shook my head. "Not really."

"Well knock it off," Jake said in a stern, parental voice. "If my experience on the street has taught me anything, it's that there is only one person with your best interest in mind, and that's you." He looked over at Harry. "Except for you, kid. You helped me out better than I could help myself. So maybe that advice is shit."

He was right. I could live a sullen life and try to make others feel badly for me. That's what I had been doing and it got me nowhere good. If I was going to change the direction of my life, it was going to be by my own volition.

Two paramedics rushed into the room. I had gotten so caught up talking to Jake that I forgot about Harry.

I stood and walked over. "I'm pretty sure he's been dead for a while."

The first paramedic through the door put two fingers to Harry's neck and waited. He turned to his partner. "No pulse." He then looked up at me. "Judging by the smell in this apartment, I would have to agree with you."

"I came over to ask him to turn down the volume on his TV and found him like this."

A police officer then entered the apartment. Thankfully, it wasn't one of the officers I had already seen in the past twenty-four hours. I could only imagine how that would look. The officer asked both Jake and I a few questions, noting them in his report, and then sent us on our way.

We walked back to my apartment.

Jake immediately went for another beer.

"Slow down, Jake." I couldn't believe those words were coming out of my mouth. I also couldn't believe I wasn't joining him. I wanted a beer. In fact, my mouth watered for its satisfying taste. I longed for the burst of euphoria that hit after downing a couple beers quickly; the lighter-than-normal feeling of a quickly fading serendipity. But Isabella's beaten face kept silhouetting itself in my mind. Her innocence seemed to drown out my desire to get drunk.

Jake looked back at me. "Listen," he said. "I appreciate your hospitality, I really do, but I don't have a lot of friends in this world. In fact, I only have one." He looked down at the newly-stocked fridge and the beer in his hand. "The booze has gotten me through some pretty tough shit. It's been the only thing to stand by my side through it all."

"I think you've got it wrong, Jake."

He put the beer back, closed the fridge, and looked at me, waiting for me to elaborate. The thing is, I hadn't planned on saying what I had. The words just once again fell out of my mouth without so much as a second thought.

"I know this is going to sound completely hypocritical coming from me, but maybe the booze is what helped to get you into all those jams in the first place. Maybe it was always there for you because it was the only thing left after everything else vanished. It was something to cling to, something that helped you to forget all the miserable things that had happened."

At that point, I didn't know if what I was saying was for Jake or me. At least for me, the booze helped me glide through life with blinders on, unable to see anything with value. It also helped shield me from the painful side of life. But as I had come to find, the painful side never goes away. It simply builds up more strongly, waiting for the right moment to pounce.

I continued. "You only have a little time left, Jake. Don't you want to make that time last as long as it can? Aren't there things you want to do with these last days?"

Jake actually looked remorseful. I figured he'd quip back with some sarcastic reply like, "What are you, a Hallmark card, kid?", but he didn't. Now I was starting to understand that he was a victim to his own inner demons, just like I was. He was gruff and somewhat calloused, but he was human. And by seeing how much he had lost, I also realized how much I had, too. In that moment, I lived vicariously through his pain and in turn shed light on pain I had set away in the attic of my memory, hoping it would never be seen again.

"I don't have anything, kid. So I don't have anything to make the time last for."

"What about your family?"

He laughed. "Trust me, they don't want nothing to do with me."

"How do you know?"

"Because they told me. That's how."

"When?"

"That doesn't matter. The words remain as true today as they did back then."

"I think it does matter, Jake." And I think I figured out what Mack wanted me to do for him. I realized I was reaching here, but winging it became the way to operate now.

He looked me in the eyes. "I said it doesn't matter. Now drop it." Jake then coughed violently. A small amount of blood trickled from the corner of his mouth.

I walked to the bathroom and brought back the same roll of toilet paper Isabella used to dry her tears.

"Here," I said, handing it to him.

He nodded his thanks and wiped the blood away. "I ain't trying to ruffle your feathers, kid. I just know that I'm not wanted." I didn't need to speculate on his feelings at that moment. The single tear racing down his cheek told me all I needed to know. "I ruined a lot of people's lives once. I won't do it twice."

I wasn't about to force what I thought was best on him. He'd just close back up like a clam. And I didn't have a lot of time to open him back up.

18

"Sean," a woman said from somewhere to my right. I tried to look, but my head was immobile.

"Sean, can you hear me?"

I wanted to reply, but I couldn't. When I tried to open my mouth, it hurt. Pain shot through my body. A loud beeping overtook all the other sounds. "Sean, wake up." I then sat upright in my bed and gasped for air as if I was drowning.

I was awake, but not free of what I just felt.

I wiped the sweat off my forehead with my hand and looked around my dark apartment. I must have been more tired than I thought to have passed out so completely. I looked over to see Jake sleeping in the chair. These nightmares had already overstayed their welcome.

I walked over to the kitchen and splashed some water on my face. I then looked up at the clock on the microwave: 6:30 A.M. Despite what I had been through, I actually felt, dare I say, refreshed. I couldn't actually place the feeling or pin it down, but something felt different. I hadn't felt that way in as long as I could remember. My head felt clearer than it usually was.

Then came the well-timed knock on the door.

Walking over, I peered through the peephole. It was Isabella.

"Hi," I said, opening the door.

"Hi, Sean," she said, handing over a round something wrapped in tinfoil. "It's raisin bread. A family recipe. It was the very least I could do."

Not wanting to be rude, I peeled back a piece of the tinfoil and picked a piece of the bread off. My grandmother used to make raisin bread for us whenever we'd visit her with my Mom. I looked forward to it. Funny, I hadn't even thought about that bread up until that moment. Somehow, it seemed a good memory had floated to the top of the murky pool of memories I usually languished in. I was sure it was soon to be devoured.

"Wow," I said, picking off another piece. "That's really good." And it was. Exceptionally good was more like it. It then hit me that I hadn't really eaten anything in the past couple of days. The stranger thing was that I hadn't felt hungry until I ate a piece of the bread. I guess I was just so caught up in the happenings of the past few days that it hadn't occurred to me to eat. Certainly not the first time that'd happened.

Isabella smiled. "Thanks again for what you did, Sean."

"It was nothing," I said nonchalantly.

"It was everything to me, Sean. You were a wakeup call I didn't expect." She then leaned across the door's threshold and planted a soft kiss on my lips. She then caressed my arm softly as if to say "thanks" without saying it.

The kiss felt amazing. It was the first kiss I'd had since my fiancée left. Or, more accurately, since I forced my fiancée out of my life. I knew Isabella's kiss meant nothing more than thanks, but the softness of her lips stayed with me long after it ended.

"I'm leaving, Sean," Isabella said. "Going to visit with my family and get back to what really matters to me. I need some time to evaluate myself. It's because of you that I can do that. Please know that."

I didn't know what to say to that. Taking a compliment was as foreign to me as speaking another language. Hell, I had enough trouble speaking English half the time. I averted my eyes and mumbled, "You're welcome."

Isabella put her soft hand beneath my chin

and slowly raised it up so our eyes met. She said, "You need to understand it, Sean. It's important you know what you've done for me. Your actions saved me."

I guess they had. I typically tried to forget a situation soon after it occurred. Not only did I not have enough space in my mind for them, but I also chose to move on quicker than most folks would, for the simple fact that most things that happened to me were bad.

I nodded and smiled, the best I could do at that moment. "When will you be back?"

"I'm not coming back, Sean."

I again nodded. It was fitting that the one person I seemed to connect with after so many years of living as a hermit would leave as quickly as she came. But I understood her reasoning and was happy she was doing it.

"I guess this is goodbye then." It felt like I'd been bitten in the gut after I said it. I didn't want to lose her, but I guess I never really had her to begin with.

"Don't worry, Sean. I may not be physically with you, but I'll always be up here," she said, gently tapping my shaggy head with her index finger.

I nodded. I didn't have the words available to express my feelings. Hell, even if I did, I wouldn't know what feelings to verbalize in the first place.

She touched my arm again and then drifted away back down the hall with a genuine smile on her face. Then she was gone. Almost as if she vanished like a ghost. Her smile made me smile, something I was unaccustomed to doing. It was almost as if my face tried to turn the smile into a frown from practice.

"What do ya got there, kid?"

I closed the door. Jake was apparently awake.

"Raisin bread." I put the loaf on the table. "Help yourself. I'm going to hop in the shower."

"Thanks, kid." He quickly dug in as I walked away.

I reached down and grabbed the hair clippers from beneath the sink. Beth used to use them to shave her poodle in the summer. She left them when she left me, inadvertently I assumed, but now they would serve a purpose. I clicked open the black plastic case holding the clippers and its attachments. Plugging it in, I then pushed it down to the lowest setting and pushed the button up. The clippers vibrated gently in my hand, steady, rhythmically.

Staring at myself in the mirror made it an easier decision.

The person that stared back suddenly made me sick to look at. How could I have let myself get so gangly and gross? I had no cares about myself. That much was obvious. But for whatever reason, I could no longer stand it. Without a second of thought I brought the clippers to my head. As close to the middle as I could get it, I pushed the clippers firmly against my scalp and eased them back until a clean spot ran the length of my head. I let the clump of hair fall off to the side and onto the bathroom floor. The air felt good against the hairless line, so I cut another swath out to its right. And then another and another until I no longer had any hair on the top of my head, aside from the few stragglers I missed on the first pass. I shored them up and then moved onto my beard. It came off with ease. My head and face, hidden beneath years of grooming neglect, now stared back at me from within the bathroom mirror. A few more wrinkles had formed during those years, hidden until now. But for the most part, this was the person I remembered me being, back before the darkness crept in.

The light over the bathroom sink popped

and went out. I reached up and tapped it, as this sometimes happened. The wiring, like the heat in the building, was a bit short of what some would call working order.

"Jake," I called out.

He didn't answer.

Then the mirror began to steam. My reflection faded out. A moment later, his face appeared, the dark man, Drake. His sickly pale face looked at me from the other side of the mirror.

"I warned you, Sean," Drake said, his words tinny and mumbled.

This can't be real, I thought. *Did I forget to take my pill?*

"You're not real," I said aloud. But if he wasn't real, then what was I seeing and hearing? Had I finally become certifiable?

Drake halfheartedly laughed. His right eye stayed partially closed. The laughing soon trailed off. "I'm as real as anything else, Sean. As real as Jake, as real as your new friend Mack, as real as your hair on the floor," he said, looking down from behind the mirror, his reflection semi translucent but fully haunting.

I closed my eyes and controlled my breathing. "It can't be real," I repeated to myself. When I opened my eyes he was gone.

The only person in the room was me, my own cleanly shaved reflection stared back.

"You alright in there?" I heard Jake ask from the living room.

"Um," is what I replied with at first. I wasn't sure what to say or how to say it. "Yes. I'm fine." I then reached over and turned on the shower's faucet. I gripped the side of the sink with both my hands, steadying myself, and closed my eyes. Whatever was happening to me seemed to be increasing. I kept my eyes closed longer than I had intended to. I was afraid of what I might see when I opened them. Much to my relief, the now-foggy mirror had no sickly man in it any longer. Only a man who saw his true self after being away for so long.

19

I took a shower that was quite possibly the longest shower of my life. The water rolled off my newly-shaved head and face. In a symbolic way, it felt like I was washing away more than dirt. Being sober for a couple of days did me a world of good. My head was clearer. I had enough brainpower to think logically and still remember the logic a minute later. But to say I didn't want a beer would be a lie. In fact, I contemplated leaving straight from the shower and cracking one open. But I held back. I wasn't ready to up and quit completely. Just like the cigarettes, I needed my vices.

My head was clearer, but that didn't mean I was better. The sickly man, Drake, appearing to me when he wasn't even physically there was a sign that my mind was deteriorating in a way I had no idea how to control. I had one thing off my plate with Isabella safely leaving town. That felt good, really good. It was probably dumb luck that I was able to help her at all. But since my luck was pretty much nonexistent, I would take it and cling to it.

Having taken care of one task, it reminded me to open the new green envelope that someone had slid under the door. I could only assume that Mack was back in town.

I sat down on the toilet with a towel wrapped around my waist, still dripping in places from the shower. I opened the envelope. No money fell out this time. That was fine by me. I had yet to spend any of the stack yet, aside from Jake helping himself for groceries.

I unfolded the note. *209 Eastman Avenue – 3:50 P.M.*

I cracked the door to the bathroom.

"What time is it?"

"2:30," Jake answered.

Plenty of time. Eastman Ave was a fifteen minute walk from my place. The sun was shining outside for a change.

"Want to get some fresh air?" I asked Jake. I didn't expect him to say yes. But I also didn't want him to think I was simply bailing on him time and again.

There was no response. I then heard the crinkle of an empty beer can. "Sure," Jake said.

20

Jake and I made our way to Eastman Avenue. The weather was abnormal for February. The sun shined down brightly through parts in the clouds, melting the upper most layer of snow to give it a glossy sheen. The temperature still sucked, though. Twenty-five degrees wasn't exactly what I would call warm, but it was better than it had been. And if I had learned anything over the years, it was to take the little things when they came.

"209," Jake said. "That's it over there." He pointed across the slushy street to the aptly named Eastman High School.

I checked my phone. 3:40. We still had ten minutes, according to the new note that Mack had left me. But ten minutes until what?

Jake plopped down on the bench at the bus stop behind us. I joined him.

"So why are we here again?" Jake asked.

"I don't know yet," I said.

Jake didn't prod. I don't think he really cared why we were there, as long as we grabbed some booze when we were done. And I'd get it for him. I debated with myself over whether I should or not. I didn't want to help him die or anything. But the thing is, and as morbid as it sounded, he was going to die soon, regardless of what I did or didn't do for him. And if the man wanted to spend his last days on Earth drunk, then so be it. Who was I to tell him what to do? I was certainly not self-righteous enough to think I was any better than him. If anything, I was probably worse in many ways.

I leaned back against the bench. "Does your family live around here?"

Jake looked at me through squinted eyes. It was evident that he didn't want me to bring that up again. But he was a grumpy old drunk. He was bound to get mad about most things. And I needed to dig deeper with him. I don't think Mack intended me to buy him beer and watch him die. That can't be why he sent me to help him.

"I told ya, kid. I don't want to talk about it."

"I'm not trying to hurt you, Jake. I'm trying to help."

"You can help by leaving it be."

"Is that helping, though?" I leaned over on the bench, putting my elbows on my knees. "Don't you want to say goodbye?"

Jake sighed and looked away. He stared out silently for a moment before saying, "I already said my goodbyes a long time ago. And trust me when I tell you this. They don't want to see me. Not now. Not ever. Hear me?"

"I hear you, Jake. But that doesn't mean I agree with you."

"You don't got to agree with me, kid."

I felt like I had to press him. "Don't you ever wonder how they are?"

"My family?"

I nodded.

"Of course I think about them. I'm not some robot. I have feelings, you know. That's why I'm not going back there. I don't give a fuck about myself. I deserve to be where I am. But I'm not putting them through it again. They don't deserve it. Now just drop it."

"Okay, okay."

I wasn't about to tie him up and drag him there, wherever his family was. Mack never said to kidnap him. Then again, Mack never said anything that didn't seem like a puzzle.

The bell rang across the street at the High School. The front doors burst open and a wave of teenagers spilled out, flooding the front of the school.

"What now?" Jake asked.

"Good question."

I stood from the bench and watched as the kids dispersed in various directions. Some hopped on buses that lined the street to the right of the school. Others were picked up by their parents, I assumed. Still others drove away in cars that were in various states of disrepair.

Seeing them drive away reminded me of my first car. It was a light-blue Ford Mustang. It was a terrible car. Not even a 5.0. But it was mine. And because of that, I loved it. My grandmother bought it for me in my junior year of high school, right before she passed. She said it was her going away present. I thought that maybe having the car would escalate me into a different social level. I was wrong. In fact, it did the opposite. I didn't have the car for long. I came out one morning to find all the windows smashed, the tires slashed, and the little hope I had of turning things around deflated.

The front doors to the school opened again. A lone boy walked out, his head down. He had a backpack on that seemed to be carrying every book ever made it was so overfilled. The boy leaned forward a bit. Otherwise, he would topple back like a turtle on its shell.

Shortly after he cleared the small flight of stairs outside the doors, a group of taller boys appeared from behind a row of hedges.

"Hey, shit stain," I heard the tallest of the boys yell. "Where you going?"

The kid with the backpack didn't look back. He didn't even acknowledge that he heard them. But he must have. I heard them from across the street.

The kid with the backpack sped up. He walked past the line of busses. He then crossed the street in front of them and walked further from the school. The three older-looking kids chased after him.

"That kid's going to catch a beating," Jake said.

That's what I thought, too. That's what we were there for. It must have been. I didn't see anyone else coming. And it was almost 4:00 by that point.

"Come on, Jake," I said, motioning for him to follow me.

We crossed the street and followed the path of the kid and his stalkers. We rounded the corner and it became clear he needed help. His backpack was already off, the zipper busted open and his books strewn across the sidewalk. A few papers were rushed away in a gust of wind, while others stayed where they fell, soaked in a puddle of melting snow.

"Let me go," the kid said.

"Hear that guys," the apparent leader of the older kids said. "Shit stain grew some balls overnight." He then pushed the kid against the chain-link fence and down into an alley that was out of my sight. The two other kids followed them into the alley.

Jake and I crossed the side street, over the kid's books, and into the alley.

"What ya gonna do, shit stain? Huh?"

"My name is Billy. You know that."

"Your name is what I tell you it is. Understand that, shit stain?" The tallest one said. He pushed Billy down onto the ground and right into another large puddle. The water splashed up as he fell, coating his back and pants in water.

I caught a glimpse of Billy's eyes. He wanted to cry. His lip quivered the slightest bit before he pursed them tight. I knew all too well how that felt.

"Hey," I said. "Leave him alone."

When I was growing up, if an adult rounded a corner while I was being an ass, I was sure to clean up my act. That wasn't the case nowadays. Kids now weren't disciplined enough. Too many parents wanted to only be friends with their kids. And that never turned out well.

"Who are you?" the tall kid asked. His buddies filed in behind him.

None of them appeared to be even remotely intimidated by me. I couldn't blame them. I was about as intimidating as a five-foot-ten teddy bear. But that didn't mean I hadn't learned anything over my own years of torment.

"Don't worry who I am," I said. "Why don't you walk away now?"

"Or what? You and your hairy friend there going to tell on us."

He laughed, which then made his buddies laugh. All the while, Billy watched from the puddle. His lips weren't pursed any longer. Hopefully, that meant that he knew he had help now. He wasn't alone.

Jake walked by me and up to the tall kid. Jake came up to about his nose.

"How old are you?" Jake asked.

"Eighteen. Why?"

Jake punched him in the gut with a lightning fast right jab. The tall kid fell to the ground like a ton of bricks. "I'm not about to go hitting a kid. But you aren't a kid. You're just another worthless adult. And if you say another word, you'll find out how adults deal with things."

The kid to the right of Jake reached for him. Jake took his arm, and like something out of a Bruce Lee movie, he spun him over onto his back and twisted his arm a little extra while he was prone to get his point across.

Jake then looked to the kid on the left. "You feeling brave, too?"

The kid shook his head almost instantly.

"Good. Now grab your buddies here and get the fuck out of my alley."

He reached down for the ringleader. "Come on, Jon. Let's get out of here."

"This isn't over," Jon said, getting back to his feet.

Jake faked a lunge towards him, making the bully flinch back, and Jake laughed right in his face. The three kids walked past us and back up the street from where they came. As Jake made sure they stayed gone, I walked over to Billy.

I held out my hand to help him up. The poor kid was soaking wet from the puddle. And although the sun was out in spurts, the temperature had already begun to whiten the thin layer of water in his clothes to ice.

"Thanks for the help," Billy said. "But they're going to make me pay for that tomorrow."

It was easy to understand why they picked on Billy. It was usually the weakest person a bully could find; easy pickings. The overly-nice kid, someone they were jealous of, anyone who looked different than them. Billy fit that mold perfectly. He was shorter than the other kids around him and a tad bit pudgy. I don't think his bright red head of hair helped his cause out any. And why anyone would let him wear Harry Potter-like round glasses was beyond me. They were probably like a beacon to a bully.

"How long have they been picking on you?"

"Forever," Billy said. "It's gotten worse lately. Ever since Jon got kicked out of school."

"Why did he get kicked out?"

Billy shrugged. "I don't know. But he's been a lot meaner since then." Billy then walked past me and back out into the side street. Jake had already gathered most of the loose papers and brought them back.

"Sorry, kid," Jake said. "These ones don't look so good." He held out the three papers that had been soaked through, water dripping from them. A large red letter A smudged in the top right corner. Apparently, the kid was good at school. Just another reason to get picked on.

"Thanks," Billy said. He bent down and gathered his books from the street, packing them back into his backpack in what looked to be the only order they would all fit.

"Can you tell the school what's going on?" I asked.

Things were also different now with the ways schools dealt with bullying. I knew that from watching the news. When I was growing up, it was seen as a rite of passage. You either endured the punishment or stood up for yourself. Now they had programs and whatnot to help. Those sure would have made my childhood years a bit easier.

"The school won't do anything about it," Billy said. "For a bunch of idiots, they are smart enough to never do it on school property."

"What about the cops?"

"My mother already went to them. They told her they had more important things to do." He shrugged his backpack on.

How Mack found these people and situations was beyond me. But I realized now why he needed me for this. The school and authorities turned their back on him. So now it was up to me to figure this mess out.

"Well, thanks again for the help," Billy said, walking away.

"Keep your chin up, kid," Jake said.

Then it occurred to me. "Billy," I said. "Do you know where Jon lives?"

"Please don't go there," Billy said. "It will only make things worse for me."

"Don't worry," I said. "I won't even mention your name. I'll say I followed them."

Billy thought about it for a moment. He then said, "He lives on Cedar Hill. I don't know which house."

"Happen to know his last name?"

"Jones," Billy said. "Jon Jones."

I guess I'd be paying the bully a visit.

21

I had never heard of Cedar Hill. That wasn't overly surprising. The city was large and had many different subsections outlying it. I had planned on going to one of the poorer neighborhoods. I had all these preconceived notions about bullies, and their upbringing and whatnot. Until about midway through high school, my life had revolved around avoiding bullies. I had a penchant for getting myself picked on. Nothing would make me happier to say I was a lover and not a fighter. But in reality, I was neither of those things. I was simply a sad little speck of a person.

"You sure this is the place?" I asked the cabbie as he pulled the car to a stop.

"121 Cedar Hill," he said. "That's it right there." He nodded out the passenger side window.

I gave him a good tip and watched the cab drive away. I had a hard time believing this was the place. There was a good reason I hadn't heard of Cedar Hill. This was apparently where the rich people lived. And 121 Cedar Hill appeared to be the largest house in the neighborhood, bordering on what I would call a mansion.

How can this be where Jon Jones lives? Maybe Billy got his name wrong. There was only one way to find out.

I walked up the long, winding driveway. I stepped up the rounded stone steps – marble I thought -- and under a portico that overhung the large double doors. From inside the house blared some obnoxiously loud music.

Is that Metallica?

I rang the bell, which was drowned out by the music.

I cupped my hands on the side of my eyes and peered in through the long piece of decorative glass beside the doors. The foyer of the house was just as large as the outside. A marble statue was centered between two ascending staircases to either side.

I stepped back and waited.

"What the hell do you want?" said someone from behind me.

I turned quickly to find Jon Jones.

He caught me off guard. "I'm here to see you, actually."

"What about?"

"Billy," I said.

"You his father or something?"

He didn't remember me. I'm not sure if that worked to my benefit or not. I sent Jake back to my place to avoid any sort of hostilities, considering Jake punched him in the gut. Now it seemed like I could have brought him.

"I'm not his father, no."

"Then why are you here? I have things to do."

"Are your parents home?" He was eighteen years old, but still living with his parents, I assumed. I doubt this kid could afford this type of lifestyle.

"Why?"

"I just want to talk to them."

"You want to tell on me? You're a little old to be tattling, don't you think?"

Maybe he did remember me. And who was this kid calling old?

"No. I simply want to talk to them. Are they home?"

Jon Jones walked past me and towards the door. "My parents are divorced. Good luck finding my father. But if you do find him, tell him to fuck off from me." He fished a house key from his pocket.

This kid was rough around the edges. No doubt about that. But he seemed bothered by his own set of issues.

"Well, what about your mother?"

No sooner had the words come from my mouth when Jon became noticeably agitated.

"I just left her. She's across the street from Meadows Field." He put the key in the door and unlocked it.

I thought for a quick second. "Wait," I said. "The only thing across from Meadows is the cemetery."

"Nice job, detective."

I felt like an ass. This kid was a bully and obviously had something coming to him. But in less than a minute of time, I found out his Dad was nowhere to be seen, and obviously not on Jon's good side, and his Mother was dead. But then who lived there?

"I'm sorry," I said. "I didn't mean to pry."

"A little late for that."

I had been so caught up in trying to do the right thing that I failed to stop and look at the situation for all it was. I instantly assumed that Billy was in trouble and it was my job to get him out of that trouble. But the address Mack gave me was simply for the school. Maybe I wrongly assumed that Billy was the one that needed help.

"Why do you pick on Billy?"

Jon opened the door a speck, enough to let the loudness of the music creep outside. He got defensive. "I don't know," he said. "Why do you care?"

"Because I was bullied growing up, Jon." He seemed a bit alarmed that I knew his name.

"So?"

"So I know how it feels when it seems like nobody cares what's happening to you. When kids you thought were your friends turn a blind eye to your struggle so they aren't the next victim. I know how it feels to run home from school every day to try and avoid a beating, or being humiliated in front of your peers. I know how it feels to cry yourself to sleep every night and dread waking up the next morning because you have to repeat the whole damn thing. That's why I care. Why do you do it? Why do you take such pleasure in hurting someone?"

I expected a smartass remark from him. Or for him to slam the door in my face. He did neither. Instead, he closed the door and sat down on the top step.

"I don't know why I do it," he said. "I'm not as much of a dick as you might think." Then he added to save face a bit, "Not that I care what you think. But Billy and I have had problems going back a few years. It's not like I pick on anyone but him."

I was geared up for a battle, either of words or fists. This sudden turn in attitude took me by surprise.

"You mind?" I asked, nodding to the other side of the step.

Jon shrugged. "Whatever."

"Thanks," I said, sitting down. "I don't know Billy. But he seemed pretty shaken up. That's no way to go through life."

The bullies in my days did it for their own reasons. It's not until you become older and have time to reflect that their motives become clearer. When I was bullied, I figured I was simply the unluckiest of all the kids. It never has anything to do with luck, or lack thereof. There is always a motive. Shit tended to roll downhill.

Jon didn't run into the house. Nor did he cop an attitude. He simply sat there with his head down.

"So, who do you live here with?"

"My stepfather," Jon said with a hint of disgust.

"Does he know you got kicked out of school?"

Jon's slouchy behavior quickly stiffened.

He looked over, nervous. "Keep it down, man. He's inside." He then looked over his shoulder at the front door before turning back to me. "You're not going to tell him, right? I mean, I'll leave Billy alone. Just don't tell him. Please."

He seemed genuinely concerned about this.

"That's not my business, Jon. Don't you think he'll find out eventually, though?"

"Not if you don't tell him. I already covered my tracks. And by the time graduation rolls around, I'll be gone."

"Where are you going?"

"Anywhere but here."

"Is it so bad here?" I looked around again at the enormous yard. Finely manicured spiral shrubs lined the driveway. Lush green lawn sprawled as far as I could see. It seemed like a good life to me.

Jon didn't say anything.

The music stopped a moment later and Jon stood.

"Shit," Jon said.

A few quick seconds later the front door opened.

A large man stepped out and smacked Jon on the back of his head. "Where you been?"

"Out," Jon replied, rubbing his head.

The large man must not have seen me at first. When he noticed me, he appeared to grow angry. "Who's this?" the man asked.

At that moment, I felt as if I put my guard down too quickly. I may not have been about to get in a fight with Jon, but the man looming over him seemed more than ready to take me up on that unsaid offer. I assumed this man was his stepfather.

"My name is Sean." I held out my hand to shake his, despite not wanting to.

His stepfather did not oblige. "And what are you doing here, Sean? This is private property."

How quickly things changed. If this had happened a few minutes sooner, I would tell this man how his stepson was a bully. That he was ruining the lives of innocent kids. That he was the scum of the Earth. But now I wasn't so sure that everything was as it appeared to be. And I wasn't about to *tattle,* as Jon put it.

"I'm here to speak with Jon."

"About what?"

I figured I might as well lie. I was getting a bit better at it. "I'm from the school." As soon as I said that, Jon seemed extremely nervous. "We were just talking about what his choices were after graduation." Kind of a lie, kind of the truth.

"You a guidance counselor?"

"Something like that."

His stepfather looked at me for a long minute. He then pushed Jon harder than a comfortable nudge should be. "Dinner will be ready soon. I expect you on time." He then walked back into the house, closing the door loudly in his wake.

Jon sighed. His face clearly showed that depression had no age boundaries. "I have to go." With his head down, Jon vanished into the house.

It became clear to me that Billy wasn't the one I was supposed to help. It was Jon.

22

I still didn't know if it was Jon or Billy that Mack sent me to help. But I figured by helping Jon, I would in turn help Billy. And the question of who to help would be moot.

I walked down the street in thought. The sun was out again. Strange occurrence for the middle of February to have consecutive nice days. I wasn't complaining. It felt nice on the little of my skin that was exposed. And now that I had a moment to myself, I couldn't help but to feel a bit clearer minded. I think part of it was not being hung-over; a feeling that was sadly foreign to me. Aside from that, I really think that helping Isabella out of her situation gave me a sense of purpose I had been lacking for a long time. But at the same time, I couldn't help but to be a bit overwhelmed by all the other problems. Maybe I had taken on too much too quickly. Maybe I wasn't ready for all of this.

Fuck.

Every time I have a glimmer of hope for myself, I burn it down with doubt. And as quickly as the good feelings came, they went.

I had told Jake that I'd pick him up some beer on my way back to the apartment. It went against my better judgment to fuel his death, but the man only had a couple of months to live. If beer made him happy, then so be it. Who was I to deny him that, simply because I was starting to see things in a new light? At best it would be hypocritical. At worst, it would push him away and I'd be further from finding out how to help.

Ducking into the package store on my right, I nodded to the clerk whom I had spoken with a few times before; the chime that hung over the door rang as I opened it. He was a nice older gentlemen who always started talking my ear off as soon as I entered.

"Nice day out there," he said.

"I'll take anything but snow." I smiled and walked down the aisle towards the beer coolers in the back.

At first, I thought about picking up a case of something foreign, knowing that Jake wouldn't drink "none of that foreign crap." That would be a roundabout way to stop him from drinking himself to death. But it seemed cruel to toy with him in that way. The look on his face as I plopped down a case of some beer he couldn't pronounce would be worth it, though.

I grabbed a case of Coors Light. I hadn't given up drinking altogether. At least not yet. What I needed to do, personally, was slow the fuck down. Having one or two beers to be social was acceptable to most of society. And that's what I needed to come to grips with. I could no longer afford, health wise, to be a drunken idiot all day and night. I knew how I felt while in those binges.

The door's bell rang out again.

My binges always started with one beer. That was always my favorite one, much like the first cigarette after not having had one in a long while. It was the rush of something different; something that helped me escape the doldrums of reality. But now that I had a chance to see what it was like without the booze – how much better I felt – it was something I was ready to give a chance, slowly.

Plopping the case on the front counter, I reached in and removed some money from my front pocket.

The usually chatty clerk said nothing. He rang me up and took the money. His hand was shaking. He seemed nervous now that I was close enough to get a good look at him.

"Is everything alright?" I asked.

Then I heard the very distinct sound of a gun's hammer being cocked. The unmistakable sound came from behind me.

I turned slowly. When I did, my nose was inches from the barrel of the gun. A man, about my height and build, stood with his hand outstretched. His face was blurred; hidden behind some kind of plastic mask.

"Your money. Now," he said.

I reached into my pocket and removed the large wad of cash that Mack had given me the last time he came by. *Why the fuck did I bring it all*? I held it out. The masked man grabbed it from me and put it in his own pocket.

And then something just snapped inside of me. It was probably the stupidest thing I had ever done in my life up until that point. And that was saying a lot. I noticed the man look away from me for a second; his eyes just white enough to see them shift behind the plastic mask. When he did, I grabbed the arm holding the gun out at me and shifted to my right. I was driven by something other than logic.

The gun fired.

The old clerk yelled and ducked behind the counter.

I instinctively moved in closer to the

gunman. We grappled down to the floor. I kneed him in his side as I had both my hands on the gun. No way in hell he was going to shoot me. A strange time to wonder it, but whatever happened to the days of gentlemen fighting with their fists to settle differences? Now everyone seemed to be carrying around a gun.

The gunman used his free hand to push my chin up. He tried to move his other hand but there was no way in hell I was letting that go.

He punched me in the gut. But I still held strong. I returned the favor by kneeing him in his side again. Once. Twice. Three times I kneed him; each one harder than the last. Then I did it a fourth time, this one closer to his kidney's than his ribs. He dropped the gun and tried to roll onto his side.

I wasted no time in sliding the gun away from him on the floor, towards the front. That's when he kneed me in the balls. A sick sensation shot up through my body, most intense in my stomach. Women had it tough; tougher than men did. I had no doubt about that. But they should all be grateful that they would never feel what it felt like to get hit in the balls. Terrible would be putting it lightly.

I fell off the man, knowing I needed to stay in the now. I couldn't let the feeling carry me away.

The man achingly began to gather himself off the floor. I rose, too. The gun was behind me on the floor. There was no way I was letting him get it. When he broke for the door, I went to grab him. He ducked, but not before I caught the thin elastic band holding his mask on, snapping it clean off his head.

Before he could turn away from me, while he was heading out the door, I shared a chilling second with him. And it was at that moment when I realized I wasn't any better than I was a few days ago. If anything, I was sicker than ever.

23

"Dr. Anders' office," Phyllis said when she answered the phone.

"It's Sean O'Rourke. Is Dr. Anders available to talk?"

"Hi Sean. He's eating his lunch at the moment. But let me check. Hold please."

I walked down the street with the phone in one hand and the thirty pack of Coors Light in the other. The clerk at the shop was so appreciative that he gave it to me free. That was good, considering the guy that robbed me got away with all my money. Served me right for carrying that kind of wad around with me. But that seemed like small potatoes compared to what I saw behind the mask.

"Hello, Sean," Dr. Anders said when he picked up the phone. "Is everything alright?"

"No, no. It's bad. Real bad. I really think I'm losing it, doc."

"Slow down, Sean. Tell me what happened."

"I went to the package store to pick up some beers."

"I thought we had agreed you were going

to try and cut back on that?"

"I was. I mean, I am. I've been doing better. But that's not the point. When I went to pay I was held-up at gunpoint."

"My God, Sean. Are you okay? Were you hurt?"

"No," I said. At least not physically. Mentally was an entirely different thing. "I was able to wrestle the gun away from him."

"Good," Dr. Anders said. He sounded genuinely relieved. "It sounds to me like you are a hero."

"Hardly a hero. But I was able to rip the guy's mask off before he ran out of the store. I only saw his face for a minute, but--" I had to say it. I mean, that's the whole reason why I called Dr. Anders to begin with. But as I remembered, a chill ran up my back. His face was the very reason I thought I needed to be taken out of society. If only I had jumped the other day, then none of this would be happening to me.

"Are you still there, Sean?" Dr. Anders asked into the silence I left him in.

"I saw myself," I said. "When the mask came off, I am sure that the guy was me. My face."

Dr. Anders took a loud breath and said, "I

see."

"Doc, I don't think you understand. I was being robbed by myself. As crazy as that sounds. The guy I fought to the ground. The guy that robbed me was me." Hearing the words solidified my own notion of craziness. How else could I explain what I saw?

"Sean," Dr. Anders said. "I need you to understand something right now. Do you trust me? Do you trust that I know what I am doing?"

I didn't distrust him. That was as good as it was going to get at that point. He never steered me wrong, but he also hadn't broken me out of my shitty turnstile. I'd give him the benefit of the doubt.

"Yes," I said.

"Good. Then I need you to accept that there is no possible way that you could be both on the giving and receiving end of what happened. Remember how I told you that traumatic events can lead to hallucinations for those suffering from depression?"

"I remember. But this was no hallucination."

"Sean. Listen to what you are telling me. You are saying that during a highly traumatic event, one in which you had a gun pointed at you, you witnessed something that goes against every fabric of what you know to be real. What is more believable: that your mind made you see something that wasn't really there due to a chemical imbalance that probably swayed too far in one direction because of the event, or that the person who held you up was really you?"

I stopped at the bench outside my apartment building, put down the thirty pack, and gave it some thought.

"Sean?"

"One minute."

What he was saying made a lot more sense than what I thought I had saw. But he said the same thing about Drake, and he turned out to unfortunately be very real. *Ask him.*

"You said that Drake was a hallucination, too."

"Who?"

"The man I saw in the stairwell in my apartment building."

"He has a name now? When you told me about him before you described him…" I heard Dr. Anders flip through what I figured was his notepad. "As short and evil looking."

"That's still true. But I've run into him again."

"Where was this?"

Then I thought about where I saw him again; at the police station. The cops didn't see him when I asked them. Maybe I was hallucinating. Maybe Drake wasn't real. But Mack said he knew him, that he was an associate of his. It hurt to even think at that moment. I had no clue what was real and what wasn't anymore. I may not have been crazy, but I certainly wasn't right in the head.

Despite my swimming thoughts, I felt myself calming down a bit.

"Sean? Are you still there?"

"I'm here. Sorry. I'm just having a hard time with all of this."

"You have nothing to be sorry about, Sean. That's why it's important that you trust me. You can't possibly know what is best for yourself at this time. But while you are unable to help yourself, I can help you. That's why you called me, right?"

It was. And the more he spoke, the more I realized that I was seeing things. But he, err, me, seemed so real. It felt like I looked into my own eyes for that split second when the mask came off.

"Have you been taking the increase in your medication?"

Shit. "No. I've just been so caught up in everything lately that I've forgotten to."

"Without your medication, these events will seem to grow in intensity. They will seem real because your mind believes them to be. I can't impress on you enough how important it is to stay on a regular schedule with your medication. You can experience very powerful withdrawal symptoms."

"You're right. I didn't even think of that."

"Good," Dr. Anders said. "Are you going to be alright, Sean?"

"Your guess is as good as mine, doc. But for the moment, I feel a bit better. I appreciate the help."

"I'm happy to hear that. If you need me, you know how to get ahold of me."

"Thanks again."

"My pleasure, Sean."

I ended the call and put the cell back into my pocket. I then looked around at the people passing me by, half expecting to see myself staring back. I didn't, though. And that was what I would hold onto for the time being. First and foremost, I needed to get up to my apartment and take those meds. I was sick of seeing people that weren't really there.

24

I knocked on my own apartment door, having given Jake the only key I had. It was Mack who opened the door.

"Welcome home," Mack said.

"Thanks." I walked past Mack and into my apartment. I put the thirty-pack of Coors Light down on the table in front of Jake. I had a feeling that he wouldn't care that they were not ice cold, a feeling I knew was right once he ripped open the cardboard case and popped open a can.

"Thanks, kid."

"You're welcome." I had to get something off my chest. "I realize this is going to sound comical coming from me, but I think you should slow down on your drinking."

Jake was in the process of downing the can of beer while I spoke. No sooner had I finished my sentence when he burped.

"I appreciate the concern. But it's not like it's going to kill me."

Being sober for the past day or two helped me see things in a different light. I liked drinking. It took the sharp edge off the days.

And I wasn't about to call it quits. Just like the cigarettes, it was something that helped me through the day. I simply needed to learn restraint. And that was going to take time. But for the first time in what seemed like forever, I was willing to give it a chance. I wanted to change, this time for the better. And while I had no intentions of becoming a hypocrite, Jake's situation was one that required me to be. It was for his own benefit.

"It is killing you, Jake. It has already killed you. What don't you get about this being your last days on Earth? Don't you have anything you want to accomplish before the lights go out? People to see? Places to visit? You can't possibly want your last days to be lived inside my shitty apartment."

Jake put the empty down on the table with more care than he had in the past few days. The gruffness he projected appeared to take a hit by my words.

I didn't want to hurt his feelings. Because no matter what, he was still dying. The last thing I wanted to do was upset him further. With having a gun pointed to my head and my own mental wellbeing coming into question, I was probably a little on edge. But I didn't want him to waste what precious little time he had left doing nothing all day. As I reasoned all of this out with myself, I couldn't help but to be a bit relived to know that I could still do that.

Jake stood from the couch. He turned to Mack. "It was nice speaking with you." He then turned to me. "Thanks, kid, for all you've done for me. You made an old man comfortable."

"Stop it, Jake," I said. "Stop running away from your problems. Is this how you've always dealt with things? When times get tough, you run away rather than deal with it?"

"I don't have to listen to this," Jake said.

"No. You don't. But I have a feeling this is what helped get you where you are. I'm not telling you this because I want grumpy old Jake mad at me. I'm not saying it so you'll run away back into the cold park across the street to live out your final few days. I'm saying it because someone has to. And right now, that someone is me."

Jake went for the door. Something came over me. I had a strong feeling that if he left it would be the final time I saw him. Then I would let Mack down. I'd let myself down.

I stepped in front of him. "Come on, Jake. I'm not asking you to stop doing anything. Drink yourself into a coma if you want. It's your life. All I'm saying is listen to what I'm saying to you. Please. Don't dismiss it. The past couple of days have been a fucking roller coaster. But I've had a lot of time to think. Don't die with regret, Jake."

The angry stare Jake was shooting me turned a bit less angry. He then backed away and sat back down on the couch. I reached over and grabbed three beers. I handed one to Mack, another to Jake, and cracked a third for myself. While I was seeing clearer, I didn't think dulling life's sharp edge would hurt all that much. I needed it.

Jake reluctantly took the can. He didn't open it.

"I didn't mean that I think you should stop drinking--"

"You're right," Jake said. His demeanor had changed. He seemed more human now; less of a sarcastic, unfeeling robot. "What you said is true. And I've known it for a while. It's easier to get drunk than to deal with my problems." He looked at me. To see tears in Jake's eyes was probably one of the most surprising things I'd seen in a while. "I figured the more I drank, the quicker I'd die. And when I was dead, then I wouldn't have to live with my mistakes any more. They are a hell of a lot worse than drinking could ever be. I need one to get over the other."

Mack chimed in. "Not necessarily true, Jake."

Jake sloppily wiped the tears from his eyes with his sleeve. He looked over at Mack.

Mack continued. "Try to think of it in a different way. If you worked through the issues, then you wouldn't need to drink to hide them. Right?"

"Easier said than done," Jake said.

"Is it?" Mack asked. "Or is the thought of dealing with the problems too much for you to handle? I can't say I'd blame you if that is how you felt. But it's important to know the distinction between the two."

I turned to Jake. "He's right. I've come to understand the same thing recently. All these years I've spent drowning my sorrows, pushing my feelings into the shadows. But the thing about sorrow is it never dies, no matter how much you drink. It is always there when you wake up. It is always there when you go to sleep." Or pass out in my case. "You can't drink your problems away. I've tried. You have to meet them fucking head on."

"And how do you propose I do that, kid? I hear what you're saying. But it's not like I haven't thought about this."

"I don't mean to interrupt," Mack said. "After all, this is not my business to intrude upon. But thinking and doing have entirely different outcomes. And at times, thinking can quietly divert a person down a road they never intended to travel. A person must act. They must do. At least then you will know if you are any closer to finding the solution for change. And change means everything."

Change. As Mack spoke, I reached into my pocket and felt the word engraved on the Zippo lighter he had given me on the Monutek roof. A strange coincidence.

My apartment fell silent.

Jake stood. "I wish you hadn't said the things you had," he said, looking at both Mack and myself.

"I'm sorry, Jake."

And I truly was. I felt bad. Maybe we poured it on a bit too thick. I couldn't speak for Mack's thinking, but I wasn't sure if another opportunity would arise to confront Jake about this stuff. It was impromptu, but necessary. I was happy it happened. But nobody liked to be ganged up on. Nobody wanted to be bullied. My mind then very quickly thought of Jon and Billy. I'd still have to figure out that mess.

"That's not what I meant. I wish you hadn't said anything because now I have to do something about it. I may be a grumpy, sour, old man, but I am that way because I let myself be that way." He walked over to the bathroom. "I'm going to need to clean myself up first. You mind if I borrow a razor and a pair of scissors, kid?"

I literally jumped out of my seat and past Jake, heading into the bathroom. That was not how I thought he would react. I thought for sure that he was gone for good this time. He was going to tell both Mack and me to fuck off and bail back out into the cold and away from his problems. I wouldn't have blamed him if he had. But he didn't. And I couldn't help but feel both relieved and genuinely happy for him.

Before I left the bathroom, I remembered what I had to do. I opened my new prescription and took my meds. No more hallucinations for me.

"Here you go," I said, handing Jake some shaving cream, a new disposable razor, and scissors. "Feel free to use this, too, if you want." I then gave him my hair clippers. Those tended to work wonders at removing thickly grown hair. I don't know how he was going to feel, but I felt liberated once I cut off my unwanted beard.

"Thanks, kid," he said. "For everything. Listen, um, will you come with me? I'll chicken out if I go by myself."

I smiled. "Of course. You know what, Jake," I said. "I think we're helping each other out."

I closed the bathroom door, feeling better about the entire Jake situation than I had since Mack gave me his name.

Mack. I'd forgotten he was still here.

I plopped myself down on the couch next to him. I picked my beer up and handed his back to him. "Cheers," I said, taking a sip. It tasted good; real good. Maybe a little too good. But at the same time, it tasted different. My first sip used to be followed by the rest of the sips in the can at once. But that wasn't who I was any longer, or who I wanted to be, anyway. I felt the desire pulling me in. A strange feeling, to say the least. The difference between then and now is I realized the pull rather than blindly allowing it to control me.

Mack followed with a sip from his can. "Care to go for a walk?" Mack asked. "The clouds sure have been clearing lately. The sun feels good."

"Sure," I said. I took another sip of beer and put the can down on the table. "Jake," I said after knocking on the bathroom door. "I'll be back soon."

25

As Mack alluded to, the nearly-cloudless sky was a beautiful shade of blue, deep and prismatic. And it actually seemed to warm up a bit since I was outside half-an-hour or so ago. It was funny in a sad kind of way. Not because of how I felt at that moment, which was fairly upbeat, but how this sort of day would have gone by unnoticed a few short weeks ago. I most likely would have either been at Monutek hating my every second there, or face down on my bed, drunker than how I was the day before.

"So, how are things going?" Mack asked as we walked down the street.

"To tell you the truth, Mack, things are going alright for a change."

"That's good to hear."

"I'm glad I didn't get up and walk out of the bar when you first offered me the job. I guess things work out how they are supposed to, right?"

"Indeed they do," Mack said. "My employer told me that Isabella is back home, healing. I figured you'd like to know that.

Without your intervention in her life, she would most likely be in a much different scenario."

"I'm sure someone would have done something. I just happened to be there for her first."

"Now is not the time for modesty, Sean. You did what others up until that point had not. You cared to help."

I guess Mack was right. It was difficult for me to accept it, though. I'd been down so deep in my emotional hole that now I forgot what other emotions felt like. It did make me happy to even think of Isabella. Her pretty face smiling at the police station once everything was over. It still made me feel good to think about it.

"And you've made amazing progress with Jake. To tell you the truth, I thought he would be quite difficult to turn around."

He wasn't the only one that thought that. And just because Jake appeared to be changing, didn't mean he actually would. I half expected to go home later to find the apartment empty and the beer gone. But if that was to happen, then I would at least know that I went past where I was typically comfortable being; I gave it my all.

"I'm assuming you found the last envelope I left for you? I slid it under your door before I had to leave town."

"I did. I'm still not sure what I'm going to do with that." And that was putting it lightly. I really hadn't given it much thought since leaving Jon's house.

"I am certain you will find a way," Mack said. "You've done well so far. How is this affecting you, though?"

"I'm okay."

Mack looked me over as we veered onto another street. We stopped.

"I have no doubt that you are okay, Sean. Most people are okay. You look much better than when I found you on the rainy roof. What I am most curious about is how you feel taking on these problems. The last thing I, or our employer, wants is for you to lose sight of your own wellbeing."

"Actually, Mack, I feel pretty good. Better than I have in a while. Don't worry about me, though." I patted him on the shoulder. "I'll be fine."

Mack smiled. "I'm sure you will, Sean." He then reached into his pocket and removed another pile of cash, neatly held together by an elastic band. "For your troubles," he said.

Mack had a great sense of need. I had forgotten about being robbed at the liquor store. There always seemed to be something going on to keep my mind distracted. I certainly wasn't complaining about that. It was nice to feel something other than depression.

I took the stack of cash. "Thanks, Mack. This job pays well, huh?"

Mack smiled again. "You'll find in time that the rewards are much greater than you could imagine."

I would expect nothing but his typical cryptic ways. I was beginning to enjoy it, actually.

"Well, I have to get going down to the Monutek building. I haven't been there in days. I can only imagine what kind of mess those people have left me."

"Okay, Mack. I'll see you soon?"

He smiled, turned, and then walked away.

I hadn't noticed, but we stopped next to The Golden Mug. I was feeling good for a change. I wouldn't have minded a beer at that point. I deserved a reward. Plus, I was going to have to eventually challenge myself to not be drunk.

26

"Hey, Sean," the bartender said.

"Hey, Tim."

"The usual?"

Nothing seemed usual about my life anymore. "Just a Coors Light, please."

The Golden Mug was as empty as ever. Only Tim and old Richard. I then did something that was completely out of character for me. I slid down to the other end of the bar.

"Is this seat taken?" I asked Richard.

He looked up with a bit of shock on his face. He then looked around the empty bar and then back to me, shaking his head softly, while at the same time motioning towards the bar stool to his right.

I sat. "I'm Sean." For all the times I had been in here, I had never introduced myself. Richard and I typically anchored either end of the bar with our own silent sadness. I didn't want to be that guy anymore, though. I felt like being personable. I wanted to open up. And before that feeling faded, I decided to act on it.

Richard shook my outstretched hand. "Richard," he said. "But call me Rich."

"Nice to officially meet you, Rich." It was more than the occasional head nod we would throw at each other.

Rich smiled briefly and then looked away from me and back down at the bottle of beer in front of him. He had chipped away at the label with his fingernails, creating a miniature army of paper crumbs on the lacquered bar top. The beer had maybe a sip or two gone from it. But even on my worst days, I knew Rich didn't come in here to drink.

"I see you in here all the time," I said.

Rich nodded sullenly and continued to chip away at the bottle's label.

Breaking the ice in a conversation was never my thing. At least not while I was sober. And it would be a lie to say I didn't consider grabbing a vodka or tequila chaser to go with my beer. I knew I'd feel looser if I went that route. But that wasn't where I wanted to be. I spent too much time already like that. I wanted to be the Sean O'Rourke I was choosing to become, and not the one I couldn't seem to escape.

I'd have to find a way to live my life without being drawn to alcohol. I had to throw away that crutch and learn to walk without its assistance. And coming into the bar would be my first test. A big test at that. Out of the frying pan and into the fire, as they say.

I took a long, satisfying gulp of my beer, but stopped myself when I typically would have finished the bottle. I put it back down and then started to scratch at my beer bottle like Richard was.

The moment became supremely uncomfortable, and it did so quickly. There I sat, in an empty bar, directly next to the only other person in there. I was minutes away from excusing myself and heading home when Rich said something that made the moment more uncomfortable, but took away my feelings to leave. I had to stay at that point.

"My wife died some years back."

He put it out in the open. Tim walked away when he heard it. I'm sure it's because at times it was only the two of them in the bar and he'd probably heard it more times than he cared to. Being a bartender didn't mean you needed to be a caretaker of people's issues. But I brought this upon myself.

"I'm sorry to hear that."

He looked up at me. "Thank you," he said. "It was six years ago. Not like it happened yesterday or anything."

"Still, losing someone you love is never

easy. Time doesn't do a very good job of healing those kinds of wounds. They lessen a bit, but never enough to really matter." I would know.

He sighed and said "That's very true. And it never gets any easier." Rich took a sip of his beer and looked around at the empty bar. "This is where we met. I was sitting in that booth over there," he said, pointing. "It was a warm summer evening when my wife leaned in over my shoulder to borrow my lighter." He had another sip of beer. "Well, we weren't married yet, obviously. We hit it off right away." He smiled, getting caught up in his own memories. "It's rare to find someone you share so much in common with. We even smoked the same kind of cigarettes. Parliament Lights."

I reached into my pocket, remembering that I still had the pack Mack had given me. I held them out to offer him one.

"No thanks," he said. "I gave them up shortly after we found out she had stage-four lung cancer. She was gone eight months after that. I know it wasn't my fault. She was a smoker long before we ever met. I can't help but to feel guilty though."

"Why do you say that?"

Rich shook his head. "I don't know. I should have been her voice of reason. I should have persuaded her to quit rather than join her. I helped kill her in a way."

"That's not true," I said. "We all make our own decisions. I've been realizing a lot about myself lately. And one of those realizations is that you can't blame yourself for things you can't fix. You can't let that sit with you and stew. All it turns into is a sticky remorse that never becomes unstuck."

"You ever lose someone to cancer?" Rich asked.

"My mother died of cancer when I was a kid. One of the toughest things I've ever gone through."

Rich looked on silently. "Aside from that, I know how it feels to lose the person you were meant to be with."

"Wife?"

"Almost," I said. "Her name was Beth. I mean, her name still is Beth." I found myself getting flustered even thinking about it.

That's when old Richard reached across and tapped his hand on top of mine. "Take your time," he said. "No judgment from me."

"She was my fiancé, and a much better person than I'll ever be. I didn't deserve her.

And I think somewhere inside of me, I always knew that."

"What happened between you two?"

"I had a small gambling problem. Actually, I was addicted to the rush. The high when I won was awesome. It was the low of losing that eventually got me. I gambled away everything I had: my retirement plan, my inheritance left by my grandfather, my dog even ran away. And then Beth finally had enough and she bailed. I came home from a night at the casino to find half the apartment empty and a note on the refrigerator."

"Geeze. I'm sorry to hear that."

"Thank you. But don't feel sorry. I had it coming. She deserved better than me."

"Well," Rich said, "for what it's worth, you seem a lot better than you do when I typically see you. You get banged-up in a hurry on most days."

"I'm trying responsibility on for size."

"It looks good on you," Rich said. He then tapped my bottle with his. "Here's to finding a better place in life." He downed the rest of his beer and tossed a ten-dollar bill on the counter. "I've got his beer, Tim." Tim nodded. "Well, I better be going. Thanks for the talk, Sean. I'll see you around."

And with that, Rich walked out the front door. And surprisingly, so did I.

27

When I stepped back into my apartment for a moment, I thought I was in the wrong place. The man that sat on the couch was not the Jake I had grown to know. His typically-unruly head of hair that usually hid beneath his worn leather cap was now parted nicely to the sides, more on the left than the right, following a thin, almost perfect line of skin across the top of his head. And his beard was gone. He looked like a new man.

"Don't you look nice," I said, teasing.

"Ah, shut up," Jake said. "It didn't feel right to put back on my dirty clothes after getting so clean and all. I hope you don't mind me going through your pile of unfolded clothes on the floor for something better to wear?"

"Not at all." I didn't have the heart to tell him those weren't clean clothes. But they were cleaner than he was used to. And he picked out the cleanest of the bunch. I saw no harm in leaving well enough alone.

Jake sat nervously on the couch. His hands were folded. "I don't know about this, kid."

"About what?"

"I haven't seen my family in five years. And the last time I did, they told me I had ruined their lives. And the thing is, kid, I did ruin their lives. I'm sure they expected me to come back at some point. Clean up my act and crawl back begging for forgiveness. But I never went back. And I don't still, which is a worse act. They aren't going to want to see me."

"You don't know that, Jake. I don't have all the answers. Hell, I don't really have any answers. But what I've found out recently is that you can't live in a world that you create; a world of endless questions and no desire to find the answers. That kind of self-destructive life consumed me for a very long time. But now I understand that in order to move away from pain, you need to confront it."

Jake pursed his lips and rocked on the couch very subtly, caught in thought. He then stood and looked me in the eyes. "Let's go before I change my mind."

And go we did. We rented a car for the day, as Jake's family was about twenty minutes away in Oakville. The closer we got to the exit, the more nervous Jake appeared to be. I drove the speed limit in the right-hand lane. As eager as I was to see this through, I wanted to give

Jake all the time available to gather his thoughts.

"You're going to be fine," I said.

"Easy for you to say, kid." Jake said as he stared out the passenger window.

He was right, of course. It was much easier for me to say that than live it. What if the situations were reversed? What if I had to confront my ex-fiancé about my own past gambling mistakes? Would I be able to do that? I feel like if I was given the opportunity, now that I was beginning to see things a bit clearer, that I may just do it. I'd tell her how sorry I was for ruining what we had. How selfish and inconsiderate I was. I'd beg for forgiveness. And if the forgiveness I looked for wasn't available, then at least I would know I tried.

"Have you thought about what you're going to say?" I asked Jake.

He nodded. "Everything I come up with is crap."

"Don't say that."

He looked over to me. "It's the truth, kid. What am I going to say that has even a bit of meaning to it? I abandoned my family when they needed me. I let my own addictions drive me to where I am now. It doesn't seem right for me to charge in here and bring all that stuff back into their lives. Aren't I doing what I did before? Putting my own stuff ahead of theirs?"

He had a point. I hadn't really given any thought to how this would affect his family. My job was to help Jake. That's what I was doing. But was this how I was supposed to help him? Getting him out of that park was essential. He'd be dead by now if I hadn't. I was fairly sure of that. And to the best of my knowledge, he wasn't the least bit drunk. No slurring, no burping, no stale beer smell to his breath. If he was ever going to conquer his past demons, then now was the time.

"What if this whole time they have been looking for you? What if they miss you? What if seeing you again changes their lives for the better? Don't dwell in the negative what-ifs, Jake. Live in the positive ones. Hope for the best. You can't change what is going to happen. But you can give it a chance to happen in the first place."

It was like someone else was speaking the words. They certainly didn't feel right coming out of my eternally-gloomy mouth. But they did. And in that moment, I felt a self-imposed burden lift off my shoulders. I felt lighter for having realized for myself that certain situations are born from life, while others are created within our minds to subdue life. I had lived in the latter for so long that it felt foreign to move towards the former.

Shit!

I swerved the rental car hard to the right. I slammed on the brakes. It was too late. We skidded into a large tree; one of many that lined the quiet suburban neighborhood.

"What the hell, kid?"

Thankfully, I was merely creeping along down the road; not fast at all. But it was fast enough to bring the car to a halt and create a large enough indentation in the hood that I'd never be able to sneak it by the rental company. But none of that mattered at that moment.

I stared at the rearview mirror as Drake slithered his way closer to the car. He was the very reason I swerved in the first place. He came out of nowhere.

I tried to turn the engine over. It wouldn't start.

Come on! I suddenly couldn't catch my breath. *Come on, fucking car!*

"What's the matter?" Jake asked.

"That guy," I said, pointing towards the back of the car with my thumb. "We need to get away from him. He's dangerous."

Jake turned around and looked out the back. "What guy?"

I looked at Jake. My eyes were wide with fear. Not only fear that Drake was within arm's reach of us now, but more so the fear that Jake couldn't see what I could. He couldn't see Drake. Which meant I was hallucinating again. Somewhere in the back of my mind, I felt like I had turned a corner, like this was behind me now.

A breakdown was coming. No doubts about it. The panic attack this time came on suddenly, unrelentingly. And I was so close to feeling good for a change. I felt like I knew what I wanted. I knew how to make things better. Then this. He shows up. And everything turns into a fucking mess.

I again looked to the rearview. He was gone. I looked to my left, then to my right. Drake was nowhere to be seen.

"Easy, kid," Jake said. "You're going to hyperventilate."

I gripped the steering wheel firmly, so much so that I felt the vinyl shift in place and crunch beneath my fearfully-tight fingers.

The hairs on my neck stood tall. When I looked to the rearview mirror again, I froze. No breath. No thought. Nothing but fear.

Drake's chillingly morbid face occupied the entirety of the mirror. He looked sicklier than before. The dark circles around his eyes were much wider now. His skin whiter and thinner, his veins creeping to the surface.

"I warned you," he said. His lips did not move, but I heard his voice.

"Leave me alone," I said.

"What are you talking about, kid? You alright?"

Drake smiled, though it appeared to hurt him to do so. "You don't know what you're doing by helping the bald man." His words dripped with animosity. "I will finish what was started. The bald man will not take you from me."

"What are you talking about?" I asked.

"You're trying to be someone you're not. You and I both know who you really are inside. You can only pretend for so long before the truth seeps back in."

"I don't know who the fuck you really are, but--"

"You know," Drake interrupted. "You've always known."

Then, in an instant, he was gone.

I closed my eyes. My breathing was out of control. I couldn't seem to slow it down.

Drake's morbid face was stuck in my mind. His words bounced inside my ears. While I could no longer see him, I could definitely feel his presence. The air still had a creepiness that it hadn't had before.

Jake touched my shoulder. "You don't look so good."

"You really didn't see Drake?"

"Who's Drake?"

"The guy standing in the middle of the road. Short guy, dressed in black. Looks like he crawled out of a grave."

"Sorry, kid. I didn't see anyone like that. You sure it wasn't a squirrel or something? Maybe a crow."

"No, Jake. It wasn't a fucking crow. I know what I saw." Or at least what I thought I saw.

Every time I ran into Drake, I began to question everything else around me. It didn't help any that I was apparently the only one that could see him. Or did I see him the first time, and every other time after that was a hallucination? I didn't know. I was beginning to think I didn't know anything anymore. What was I doing, trying to help people with their lives? What kind of right did I think I had doing these things? I was sick. I was demented. I was totally losing my fucking mind.

Jake smacked me lightly against my cheek with the back of his hand. "Kid. Snap out of it. You're starting to scare me."

I shook it off. My mental health aside, I had crashed the car into a tree. One thing after another, and always at once.

I tried to start the car again. No luck. And the tiniest bit of steam rising from beneath the crumpled hood led me to believe I had busted the radiator. Even if the car did start, we weren't going anywhere in it.

Jake got out and walked around to my side. He opened my door and stood there with his hand out. "Weren't you the one who just told me that we can't change what's going to happen?"

My breathing had slowed a bit. Enough to feel semi-normal again. I looked up at Jake. The clean Jake I had helped him become. The man who was on his way to face the worst decision he had ever made. I wouldn't let my worsening insanity ruin that. Not when we were so close to helping him move past this.

I took his hand. "You're right." He helped me from the car. I was not going to let Drake, or whatever it was I kept seeing, stop Jake from following through. "How far is your house from here?"

"It's that brown one down there." He nodded. "The one with the lemon tree in the front yard. That *was* my house, anyway. Don't know if my family still lives there or not."

"Let's go find out."

28

We stopped behind a large oak tree on the corner before Jake's house. Now that we were this close, Jake seemed reluctant to move the final few steps. He stood with his back to the tree, his house on the other side.

Even though my mind was swimming with thoughts of the sickly man named Drake, I knew I had to help Jake through this moment.

"You can do this." I said for reassurance.

I wanted Jake to know that I was there, and he wasn't going about this alone. But in all reality, I had no idea if Jake had inside of him what it would take. I tried to put myself in his shoes. It wasn't too much of a stretch. I knew how it felt to lose so many things you loved because of some monumentally bad decisions. But forcing him forward felt like forcing myself. And I didn't like it any more than he seemed to. But in this instance, I'd do what I had to; I'd live vicariously through Jake and help him all that I could.

"I don't know if I can go through with this," he said, shaking his head. "I thought I could. It seemed like the right idea before. But now that I'm here…"

I knew at that point that I could no longer be casual about this upcoming encounter. I couldn't afford Jake the opportunity to run away from it. It seemed like he was inching closer to that by the second. I knew that if it was me in this position that I would be the same way.

"I'm going to knock." I then began to walk away, slowly, towards the house. I hoped my ruse would work on Jake. I didn't want to knock on that door. What in the world would I say? I simply wanted to jumpstart Jake's stalled motives.

"Please don't," Jake said, almost begging.

"Then come with me." I kept walking. I waved for him to join me. He needed tough love. "This is your chance, Jake. Don't live in regret any longer than you have to. Now is your time to change."

Change. I felt for the Zippo in my pocket.

Jake looked down at the ground. His face told the story of a man battling his own inner demons. I knew the face because I made it quite often. He then pursed his lips again, whitening the wrinkles around his lips. "I'm coming. I'm coming."

We approached the poured-concrete front

walkway. Jake tried to smooth out the wrinkles in the clothes he borrowed. He made sure his perfectly parted hair had stayed that way. He reached the front door, stopped, gulped, and then rang the doorbell.

I thought for sure we were going to have to have another pep talk. He apparently had other ideas.

He took a large breath and held it, releasing the air in tiny, well-timed shorter exhales.

A woman answered. She was on the phone. I heard her say as the door opened, "Can you hold on a minute, Janice? Someone's at--" That's when she dropped the cordless phone from her hand as if she'd been shot. The crash knocked the battery from its rear compartment and sent it shooting across the hardwood floor and out of sight.

The woman stared out through the screen door, her mouth agape.

Jake gulped again. "Hello."

The woman did not flinch. She did not move. It was as if she'd been turned to stone with wide-eyed shock stuck on her face.

"Mom, who is it?"

And when the young woman, maybe in her early teens, came to the door she, too, froze like a statue. Both of them captive to a moment they undoubtedly did not expect.

"Hello, sweetheart," Jake said. His lip quivered. A gasp shot from his mouth. He then began to cry. Standing, slouched, and heaving in an emotional pain he had obviously walled-off for the past five plus years.

"Dad?" Her own lips began to quiver. "Is that really you?"

Jake nodded. He closed his eyes for a moment, forcing the build-up of tears to stream down his cleanly-shaved face. He crumpled to his knees, but never took his eyes off the door. "I'm so sorry," he said. "I'm so very sorry for what I've done to you." Those were the only words he could speak before becoming consumed and overwhelmed by the moment.

I wanted to say something. I felt like I should at least introduce myself. I was, after all, just standing there, watching a private moment transpire in public. It didn't feel like my place to be, let alone gawk.

"Get out of here," Jake's wife said. She, too, began to cry. "How dare you bring misery back into our lives. The past five years have been torture. Where have you been, Jake?" She sobbed more. "Where have you been?"

"Ma'am," I said. "If you just--"

"And who are you? One of his gambling buddies? Or are you one of his drinking buddies? Either way, you're not welcome here." She went to close the door. "Neither of you are."

"Jake's dying," I blurted out. I'm sure that's not how he wanted to break the news. Especially in front of his daughter. And I don't think he envisioned me being the one to do it. But Jake was too emotional to stop the door from closing in more ways than one. I had to act on his behalf.

She stopped closing the door. "What did you say?" she asked me. Her tone had gone from one of anger to that of a caring confusion.

Death had a way of doing that. Anger could be quickly displaced when the situation left it with little choice.

I looked at both his wife and daughter. "I said he's dying. And he doesn't want to do that without trying to fix his biggest regret. He knows what he lost. And all he wants is for you to know that, too."

His daughter stared at me. I looked into her eyes and saw the pain that Jake had caused her. I relived in that moment the past five years, during which the person she loved more than anything wasn't there for her. The person who couldn't see what he had right in front of his eyes. The person that selfishly put himself above all others. And then I saw those feelings vanish in that instant, replaced by a daughter who missed her father.

His daughter opened the screen door slowly. The figurative barrier holding Jake's mistakes in had been broken. She slowly took one step outside. Her mother gently grabbed her by the shoulder.

"It's alright, Mom," she said. She smiled and then turned back to Jake, who was deflated on his knees before her; a sinner ready for his long overdue penance.

Jake's daughter stood before him. She looked down at him for a second and then cupped his head in her hands and pulled him close to her, hugging him the best she could from her position.

I had never in my life heard a grown man weep so openly and strongly before that moment. It was so powerful that my own eyes teared up. His love for what he lost and what he found again exuded from his every pore. I felt it wash through me as if I was Jake and his absolution was also mine.

"I'm so sorry, honey," Jake said. "I'm so, so

sorry for what I've done to you." He looked up to his wife, Sarah. "What I've done to your mom. I was sick. I am sick. But I'm seeing clearly for the first time since I left." His head sunk further in her embrace. "Please forgive me, sweetheart. I beg of you."

"I forgive you, dad." She put her head on top of his and they cried together.

Jake's wife still seemed shocked at what had just shaken her afternoon.

"Are you okay?" I asked her, my voice low as to not interrupt what was happening with Jake and his daughter.

Jake's wife played with the necklace around her neck. She stared at her daughter, embracing the father that had left them five years prior. She then turned to me. "How do you know Jake?"

The truth would suffice. "I found him in the park. He's been living there for a long while now."

She turned back to look at Jake. "How long does he have?"

"The doctor said maybe two months. Probably less."

She studied the moment for another minute or two. She reached for the handle to the screen door but backed away. Her hand

and mind were in an obvious disagreement.

"I know you don't know me from a hole in the wall," I said. "And I don't pretend to understand what happened between the three of you. But I've had my fair share of problems, too." It felt liberating to say *had*, rather than *do*. "So I know how painful what he did was. I hurt a lot of people myself. I lost the love of my life because of it." And so many other things. "But at the same time, I know how terrible he feels for the mistakes he's made. He knows what he's done. He knows he can't take it back. But I think we all need to search our hearts now and again to find a way past the mistakes that block us from righting them. I know now how important it is to even understand that. Please. I'm not asking you to give him another chance or anything like that. But I am asking, from one broken person for another, please don't turn your back on him like he did to you. Don't let him die alone and regretful."

She again reached for the door and this time followed through. She looked at me, her eyes watery, but not yet tearing. She then seemed to drop the stonewall she set up to guard herself and brushed past me.

Jake stood, his arms by his sides. His face was more wet than dry.

His wife then hesitantly took another step, and another, until she was within arm's reach. Jake and his wife stood near one another, with a couple feet of doubt and five years of uncertainty separating them. His wife then reached in and hugged him, cautiously at first, lovingly soon after. His daughter joined them.

I watched silently as Jake's greatest fear – that of having to deal with his largest mistake – washed away in the moment. I have to say that it felt great to see such a tormented man be able to see even the slightest reprieve before he passed.

Jakes wife and daughter welcomed us into their home for coffee. Jake recounted the past five years to them; most of which consisted of regret, booze, and very cold winters. The longer he spoke, the closer they moved towards him both in proximity and in acceptance. He learned that his daughter was quite good at the piano now. She was in the top of her class academically. But what brought Jake to tears again was the scrapbook his daughter made after he left. Drawings, movie stubs, notes, anything to do with Jake was in it. She told him that even while he was away, he was always her father and she always thought of him. It touched me deeply.

Mack hired me to help people. And that's what I was trying to do to the best of my abilities. But in the process, I was helping myself. Maybe that was what Mack meant when he said this job would be worth more than I would know.

Jake's wife and daughter agreed that his final days should be at home with them. They could rekindle what they had, and share what they missed of each other's lives. Addiction would eventually claim another victim. There was no stopping that now. And his family knew that they would need to say goodbye again in a short amount of time. But at the very least, he could die at peace with himself, with the understanding that life rarely goes the way we want it to.

And that was how I left him. Happy for a change and in a life without regret. He had his faults, but deep down he was simply a broken, sad man who needed someone to help him realize he had a lot to live for.

The next time I saw Jake was at his funeral.

29

I was in the nightmare again. Bound and unable to speak. It differed a bit this time. It wasn't as dark as it was before. This time, I saw a very dim circle of light above me. I tried to focus my eyes to get a better look. No matter how hard I tried, the light did not sharpen at all, still hazy and unfocused. It was impossible to tell what it was, or for that matter, where I was. I felt no heat from the light. And it did not hurt my eyes to look directly at it.

Then voices. I don't know if they were the voices from before. They did sound clearer than I remembered them being. I was close to certain that it was two men and two women. No, three women. A bit of mumbling. *Is someone crying*? I know that cry.

I waited for the jolt that I had typically been getting at that point in the nightmare. None came. The crying continued.

"Please give him more time."

I knew that voice, but couldn't place it exactly. But what did that mean? Give who more time? Was I supposed to know what this was about? Was this about Jon? Jake? Who was

I to give more time?

"There is not much time left to give, I'm afraid."

Who is that? I heard my voice, but I'm certain my lips did not move. I didn't recognize that last voice. It was a deep man's voice; one I had no memory of ever hearing.

I heard more crying. The same woman I believe. I was tired of hearing crying. It rarely meant good things.

I tried to move my arms. I couldn't feel my arms; it was the same with my legs.

Hello? Why can't they hear me? I'm ready to wake up now.

"You'll need to make the decision soon."

What decision? Hello?

More crying bounced around the room. Then it felt like someone touched my chest. It felt nice, warm. *Who is that?*

Then there was a knock. *What's that*? It was loud, familiar. Another knock, and another.

"Sean."

Then another knock.

My eyes sprung open. I sat up in my bed.

Another knock.

"Sean. Are you home?"

I looked to my clock. 10:00 A.M. I rubbed my eyes. I figured I hadn't adjusted to being awake yet. But even after rubbing my eyes and taking another look, the date on my clock was a bit more than a month past when I last looked at it. That, of course, was impossible. There was no way a month had passed. My clock was apparently breaking down, just like everything else around me.

Even though I woke from the nightmare, I was not dripping in sweat as I was in the past. The nightmare was unnerving. It lingered in my mind, creating questions that I didn't have the capacity to answer.

Another knock. "Sean?"

It was Mack. I went over to the door and opened it.

"Where have you been?" Mack asked. He looked concerned.

"What do you mean? I've been right here. After I dropped off Jake, I came home, watched a bit of TV, and then I went to bed."

"I haven't heard from you in well over a month, Sean. I've come by daily to check on you, hoping you would turn back up. I was worried."

"Come on, Mack. Very funny." Mack didn't laugh. He didn't smile. Then I remembered my alarm clock. Then I smiled. "You went out of your way to fool me, Mack.

Nicely done. Kind of creepy to know you snuck in here to change my clock while I was asleep though."

"I assure you, Sean, I did nothing to your clock." Mack then walked past me and angled himself to get a better look at the clock beside my bed. He then stepped back, pondering something that brought a crease of wrinkles to his forehead.

"Wait. You're serious? You didn't do this?"

Mack shook his head. He still seemed lost in thought. "I have to attend to a few things. I'm glad you are alright." He turned to leave.

"Wait," I said. "You're just going to leave?" The whole clock thing bothered me. But I obviously hadn't been in my bed for the past six plus weeks. That was an impossibility. I'd be long dead without food or water. Sadly, I think I was becoming used to my crazy-tinted world. The sickly man, the inaccuracies, the overall strangeness of it had lost a bit of its bizarre luster. I wasn't complaining. I'd rather be used to the crazy than re-experience it over and over.

Mack turned to me. "I have some rather urgent business I need to address right away. I'm glad to see you are no worse for the wear." He turned to leave as quickly as he arrived. But before he left, he asked me how everything was coming along.

"Great, actually. Isabella is safe. Jake is home." Then I thought of Jon. I still hadn't given him much thought. I'd have to change that.

"Good," Mack said. "I will need you to complete any outstanding problems as soon as possible. Our employer needs them done right away."

"Can I ask why he needs this sped up? I thought I was doing a pretty good job of things."

"You are doing a remarkable job, Sean. But time is now of the essence."

"Why all the secrecy, Mack? Don't you trust me after all I've done?"

"It has never been a matter of trust, Sean."

"Then what is it, Mack? I'm the one putting myself out there. I'm doing everything you've asked of me. It doesn't seem right to keep things from me at this point."

Mack looked me straight in the eyes. "Sometimes we do things that don't seem logical at the time. But in hindsight, everything will become clear. We are nearing that point, Sean. I simply need you to keep doing what you've been doing. I'll take care of the rest."

I turned from the door, frustrated. I hoped the clock would tell a different date when I looked again. It did not. I wasn't going to get any more out of Mack. I knew that. And, anyway, when I turned back, he was already gone.

30

I showered and shaved. It felt good to be clean. I had forgotten how cleansing a good shower could feel. No sooner had I put on a pair of jeans and a shirt when another knock sounded. This one was softer than Mack's banging. I was a popular guy all of a sudden.

I opened the door.

"Hello again, Sean."

It was Jake's wife, Sarah.

"Hello," I said.

She came right out with it. "Jake passed away last week."

A deep feeling of sorrow overcame me. Something pushed that sorrow to the side. It was a realization. I had just dropped Jake off yesterday. Unless the clock was somehow right and it was six weeks later. But that was impossible. It was one of the moments when I had too much to consider at once. My mind simply went blank.

"I've come by your apartment a couple of times over the past few days. I could never seem to catch you at home."

"When did he die?"

"This past Friday," she said. "He passed in his sleep, peacefully. And thanks to you, at home."

I knew I shouldn't ask this question. "What day is today?" It made me appear like the loony person I felt myself becoming. But I had to. I had no idea which way was up at that moment.

She seemed unnerved, but answered all the same. "Today is Wednesday."

Wednesday? I think it was time to take up Dr. Anders' offer to change my medication. I don't think the one I was on, no matter the dosage, was working the way it was intended to. I dismissed the thought for now. It was doing neither of us any good for me to stand there like an idiot and talk to myself.

Then the sorrow reminded me that it was there.

"I'm sorry for your loss," I said. It was what people said at uncomfortable times like that. That's why I said it. I felt like it was as much my loss as it was hers. I knew that wasn't even remotely true. They had a wonderful life together before their world fell apart. But I had grown to really like Jake.

"Thank you," she said. "For your words and for bringing him home to us. I hated him from the point when he left us to the moment I saw him outside my door. Years of empty hate. If it wasn't for you, he would have died with me hating him for something he didn't even know controlled him. I was never going to give him another chance. But I'm glad you put that chance in my lap. When you saved him, you saved us all. And I can't thank you enough for that."

I smiled. That made me happy to hear.

"I've come to ask a favor," Jake's wife said.

"Sure. Anything."

"His funeral is today. Emma is downstairs waiting for me in the car. Would you come with us to Jake's burial? He wanted it small, no mass. But he insisted that you be there. He said not to take no for an answer." Then she said bashfully, "He said you were stubborn."

I'm stubborn? He poked me even in death. "Of course," I said. "I wouldn't want to miss saying goodbye."

I had no idea where my suit was. I rushed to the closet on the other side of the room and started to push my clothes aside. I looked for the plastic bag from the cleaners. I rarely had to wear a suit. I think the last time was at my job interview for Monutek. So after that, I tended to get it cleaned and store it away. That was pre-depression. But I didn't see the plastic bag, which made me wonder if I had ever picked it back up.

I turned. "I can't find my suit."

"Oh," she said. "Please don't get dressed up. You being there is all he wanted."

I nodded. "Fair enough. Just give me a couple minutes to put something better than this on." I looked down at my jeans and t-shirt.

She reached out and touched my arm gently. "Take your time. We'll be waiting outside." She then walked from my front door and back down the stairwell.

I rummaged through my clothes. Jake looked like shit when I met him. I wasn't going to look like it when I said goodbye, though. I found some nicer pants, pleats and all. And the button-down shirt that went with the suit I couldn't find. That would do. I then put on a tie and headed downstairs to say goodbye to the first new friend I had made in a long time.

31

The only cemetery in town was across from Meadows Field. It was a rather large cemetery. That in itself didn't seem to mix well with being across the street from the largest Little League ball field in the town. It was a strange paradox. So much youth directly across from so much, well, death.

We arrived at the cemetery. The casket had already been put neatly atop the newly-dug hole in the ground. The ride over with Jake's wife and daughter had been fairly silent. There wasn't much any of us had to say to the other. Our only connection was a man we were on our way to bury. But it was a cordial silence.

I was surprised by the amount of people that showed up for Jake's funeral. I knew Jake as a dying homeless man. These people knew him as he was before that. They remembered the man I never had the pleasure to know. It was nice to see.

After the minister finished with his quick service, Jake's wife turned to me.

"Would you like to say something?" she asked.

My first inclination was to shake my head no. I hated speaking in front of people. This was especially true when I barely knew the subject. In this case, Jake. But an urge drove me to go against what I wanted to do, and do what I know I needed to.

"It would be an honor," I said.

I walked over to the podium that rested atop a small pedestal with a green lining. The eyes of the mourners followed me. I walked slower than I normally would have. I tried to think of what I was going to say. I had grown to know him a bit since pulling him out of the park that one early morning. But I didn't really *know* him. Then again, while I didn't know all his likes and dislikes, I knew the man he was. I figured that I would speak to that.

I cleared my throat.

"Thank you," I said, the microphone spitting a bit of feedback into the air. I cleared my throat again. "Thank you for coming to see Jake off." *Oh God. See him off*? It's not like Jake was going on a cruise. Panic tried to set into my mind, but I quickly told it to fuck off. I was tired of it getting the better of me. I had to say goodbye to a friend. And that was what I was going to do.

"I didn't know Jake for all that long. The

first time I met him, he punched me in the face." The gathering of mourners laughed at that. I realized that I could have started better. I wanted to stick to it, though. What better way to honor him than by being truthful? "He was grumpy, brash, and stubborn to the core." Jake's wife then looked to me in confusion. This obviously was not the way most eulogies went.

I continued. "I'm not saying this to tarnish anyone's memory of Jake. I say this because it's the truth. I say this because Jake helped me realize that we all have problems of our own. Some of us are better equipped to deal with those problems than others. The reason Jake and I got along so well was because we both failed at confronting those problems before they spiraled out of control. But does a man's worth lie in his mistakes? I don't think so. A person should be remembered for who he was at his core, shouldn't he? The person most of you likely still see in your head."

I looked around as I spoke. Some people slowly nodded, while others trained their unbreakable stares at me. I didn't mind. I wasn't there to appease them.

"Beneath his gruff exterior, Jake was a loving soul. He loved his wife and daughter more than words could ever say. I was fortunate enough to see that love spill freely from within him. But loving souls can sometimes be the most tormented. Loving souls are more susceptible to interference, more prone to mistakenly suck in something unwanted and hold onto it. And sometimes, it's that vulnerability that's our greatest weakness."

I didn't mean to say *our* greatest weakness. I was speaking about Jake. The more I spoke, the more I realized that Jake and I had more in common that I first thought. I suddenly felt like I was eulogizing the both of us at that moment.

"Addiction, depression, anger, sadness. Anyone of those can lead a person off their intended course in life. Combine two of them and the person you thought you knew becomes someone you no longer want to know. Put them all together, and you find yourself alone. And being alone is the worst punishment, the worst retribution imaginable. Because when you are alone with those emotions, all a person can do is dwell on what got them there and lament not having a way out."

When I said that I'd speak, I had no clue

this was going to come out. Honestly, I had no idea I even had it in me to begin with. But they came flooding out of my mouth. Realizations I didn't even know I knew.

I looked over to Jake's closed casket. "There lies a great but tormented man. A man who, in the final days of his life, found a way out of his personal darkness and back into the light where he rightly should have been. I will miss Jake." I looked around, stopping when my eyes set on Jake's wife and daughter. "And I'm sure all of you will too. But I ask you to please remember the man before the torment stole who he was."

I wanted to say more, but I didn't. I said what I needed to, more than I intended to. I left myself kind of numb.

"Thank you." I then stepped from the podium.

I smiled humbly at Jake's wife as I walked closer. She pulled me in and pecked me on the cheek.

"That was perfect," she said.

I stood in the back, behind his family. The minister closed out the proceedings and the gathering of people slowly disbursed.

I looked over at Meadow's Field across the street. The days were warmer now. The snow was thankfully long gone. The sun beamed down from behind slowly moving clouds. As I looked back, I caught site of Jon, the bully. He sat in front of a grave with his head down. It seemed odd how that fell into place. I remembered him telling me how his mother was buried here. Of all the times to see him, now was peculiar, but fortuitous.

I said my goodbyes and told Jake's family that I needed to go for a walk and that I wouldn't need a ride back to my apartment. I had one last thing to attend to. And according to Mack, I needed to do it right away.

32

"Hey, Jon." He looked at me as I stood over him. He clearly did not remember who I was. Nor do I think he expected company while on a private visit with his mother's grave. "I'm not sure if you remember me or not. I came to talk to you at your house," I wanted to say a couple of days ago, but was it only a couple of days ago? According to my clock, time had shifted forward six weeks while I slept. Thankfully, that seemed to jar his memory. I wasn't forced to put my insanity into a timely context.

"Oh, yeah," he said. "What do you want?"

"Nothing, really. I noticed you over here. Figured I'd come by."

"Why?"

It was a good question. I lacked a good answer.

Then he asked, "What are you doing here, anyway? You like hanging out in cemeteries or something?"

"No. I hate cemeteries, actually. I know too many people in them. Remember that guy who punched you in the stomach?"

"Ya. I better not see that guy again. Or else me and my buddies are going to give him some pay back."

"Well," I said, "you won't have to worry about him. He's over there." I pointed to where the cemetery staff was lowering Jake's casket into the ground. I watched for an extra minute until it was out of sight. *See ya, Jake.*

"How did he die?" Jon asked.

"Cirrhosis."

"What the hell is cirrhosis?"

"A disease you get from drinking too much alcohol. He basically drank himself to death." It was a harsh but good lesson for someone of Jon's age to learn.

Jon shrugged it off. "Sorry about that," he said. "I know how it feels."

Grace Williams was the name carved on the tombstone. "That your Mom?"

He turned to me and nodded.

"I lost my mother when I was thirteen. Not a day goes by that I don't miss her."

Jon stood. "How did she die?"

"Cancer," I said. One monster got her before the other could.

"How did your Mom pass?" I asked.

"Car accident. Drunk driver." Jon reached out and gently touched the gravestone. "I come here a lot. I like to talk to her, even though she can't talk back. You ever do that?" The look in his eyes told me that he needed reassurance that it was normal to speak with those who can't answer back. "With your Mom, I mean?"

"Talk to her?"

He nodded.

"Sometimes. I used to a lot more than I do now. I just haven't been myself lately. I think about her a lot, though. Life was better when she was around."

That seemed to make Jon sad.

"Does your stepfather come here with you?" I asked.

"No," Jon said. "And it's better that way. I don't think my Mom would like who he's become."

"How so?" I realized at this point that I was overstepping my bounds. I was surprised that Jon was speaking with me as candidly as he was, especially in the middle of a cemetery. Now I was trying to drag his deep emotions out into the open. What I hoped to accomplish was beyond me at that point. But if I didn't try, then I wouldn't know. "It's okay," I said, sensing Jon's reluctance. "It's none of my business. You looked like you could use someone to talk to is all."

"I gotta get going," Jon said as he began to walk away.

"You need a lift or anything?" I didn't have a car. But I'd grab us a cab if need be.

He shook his head and slumped away. I watched as the problem I so desperately needed to fix disappeared into the street.

33

My night's sleep was great for a change. The first night I could remember that I hadn't been tormented by things I couldn't understand. I woke that morning feeling refreshed, ready to take on the challenge of understanding Jon.

I decided to head down to Eastman High again. I didn't feel like going back to Jon's house was an option at that point. His stepfather didn't want me there. And I wasn't so sure that Jon wanted me there. But as strange as it was, this was my job. I had to dig into Jon's life to find out how to fix it.

I waited until the end of the school day. I sat on the same bench that Jake and I sat on the first time we went down there. I scanned the bushy area across the street; the one where Jon and his buddies hid to ambush Billy that first day. I didn't see them.

The school bell rang as it did before. The children all flowed out of the double doors as they did before. And just like I had rewound the situation, Billy came fumbling out of the school with his overly-huge backpack.

Still no Jon.

I walked across the street and met Billy.

"Hey, Billy. Remember me?" I said and instantly knew that I sounded like a creepy guy that lurked around the school.

Thankfully, he did remember. "Oh, yeah. I remember. Where's your friend?"

"He died," I said. There was no sugarcoating death.

"Sorry."

"It's alright. He's better off this way." There was a quick moment of uncomfortable silence. "How are things going with you?"

"Better. Jon hasn't bugged me since that day you guys showed up." He thought for a moment. "Actually, I haven't seen him at all since then. Can't say I miss him much."

That was good news. To save even one kid from bullying was a win in my book. But Mack said that I'd know when I finished one of the jobs. And he was right. I knew with Isabella. I knew with Jake. But I didn't have that same feeling at that moment. My earlier hunch appeared to be right. I was supposed to help Jon. Billy being rescued was a great side effect of that.

"Have any idea where I can find him?"

"Not really," Billy said. "We don't really

go to the same places."

I figured as much.

"Well, thanks, Billy."

Billy nodded and walked away, vanishing down the same street where I watched him get attacked by Jon and his buddies.

34

"Are you a psychic or something?" I asked, taking a step up the stairs to my apartment building.

There was Mack, like a magician, appearing out of nowhere. I needed to speak with him desperately about Jon and how I was having problems with solving his issues. Maybe that was how he seemed to know so much about everything, myself included. Was Mack magical?

He laughed. "No. I'm afraid I have no special powers. Just intuitive is all."

That was putting it mildly.

"I think I'm going to need some help on Jon," I said. "I'm not sure what I can do for him?"

"I wish I could help you complete it, Sean. I really do. However, these tasks need to be done by you alone."

"Why is that, Mack?" I had asked him before. I doubted I would get any less than the same roundabout answer I typically got.

"Because, Sean, these issues are not mine to intrude upon."

"But they're mine?" I couldn't understand how it wasn't Mack's business, but it was mine. If this guy paying me to do this really wanted these folks to be better, then why not use every resource available to him, such as Mack? It seemed counterproductive to force me to muddle through them when I had no ideas. But I knew if I asked that I wouldn't get much of an answer.

Mack seemed to be struggling with something at that point. It was like he wanted to tell me something but couldn't. In fact, I felt like that's exactly what it was.

"You will need to solve this now," Mack said. He sounded alarmed. "I suggest you take it head-on. Our time is running out."

Time is running out? I knew I had heard that recently. Then it hit me: my nightmare. Someone said that time was running out in my nightmare. Was it coincidence?

"I've tried to speed this up, Mack. I saw Jon yesterday at the cemetery. He seems like a normal hormonally-challenged teenager. He's not bullying Billy anymore. I don't see what I'm supposed to do."

Mack stopped and walked a few steps closer to me. "Look deeper, Sean. Find out why Jon was bullying people in the first place. I believe that is where your answers are." He placed his hand firmly on my arm. "Find what he has buried. You need to find what he doesn't want you to."

"As in people?"

"No." Mack pointed to his head. "Find what he's buried up here."

"Why all the urgency, Mack?"

"Because a life is at stake, Sean. You need to hurry." He then turned and disappeared into the crowd on the sidewalk.

35

A life is at stake? Who says that and walks away? *Mack, that's who.* It didn't leave me feeling all that great. But it did light a fire under my ass. If Jon's life was at stake, then I knew I needed to find him in a hurry. The first place I was going to look was the last place I wanted to: his house. And that meant I was probably going to have to deal with his stepfather again.

Out of all the cabs in the city, it was strangely the same cab driver that dropped me off at Jon's house again. I told him he didn't need to wait. I had no idea how long I would be there. I walked up the long, slinking driveway again and up to the front door. There was no loud music blaring like the last time. It almost seemed too quiet.

I walked to the front door. Before I could ring the bell, Jon answered, shirtless and surprised.

"You again?" he said with fear in his eyes. "Now's not a good time."

"Hey, Jon. I just want to talk."

Jon looked quickly over his shoulder and back into the house. "I don't think that's a good idea."

"Why not?"

"Larry doesn't like me talking to other people."

I figured Larry was his stepdad. "Why is that?"

Jon stepped further onto the front steps, closing the door until only a sliver of light was left. "He just doesn't."

I knew turmoil and lies probably better than most. And I knew that he was doing one because of the other. Mack told me I needed to act fast on this. I had to push. I had to pry. I wasn't there to make friends. I was there to help save a life.

"I know you're lying, Jon. I know because I can see pain on a face from a mile away." I needed to be more drastic about this. "Listen, Jon, there was a time not too long ago when I tried to kill myself."

Jon closed the door the rest of the way. He nodded for me to follow him around to the side of the house.

"Dude, why are you telling me that?"

I knew from experience that when a person offers up something as drastic as that, the other person may be more prone to revealing something about themselves. I'd make myself vulnerable so he didn't have to be the only one.

"I want you to know who you are talking to. I'm not your stepfather. Or anyone of authority. I'm just a guy trying to help you out."

"I don't need any help, man. And you really need to go," Jon said. "If Larry finds you out here, he'll get his gun. He'll say you were an intruder or something. He's done it before. He's dangerous."

At that point, I just didn't care. I was sick and tired of being afraid. The world was no less scary today than it was the day I tried to kill myself. The difference was my attitude. I felt lighter and freer to think on my own, less clouded and subdued.

"Why are you so concerned with him finding us? All I want to do is talk."

"I told you. He doesn't like people in his business. Please go before it's too late."

Too late for what?

"Well, is he home?" I asked.

A fearful look swept over Jon. "Ya, man. But please, just go."

I could feel the invisible clock ticking. There wasn't time to think this through. I needed to go on my gut. And my gut was screaming at me to do what I didn't want to.

I walked by Jon. He tried to stop me by grabbing for my arm, but I went by too quickly.

"Stop," he said as I pushed open the door. "You don't want to know."

But I did want to know. "Larry," I shouted. "I need to speak with you."

"Please," Jon said. "Let it stay buried."

Stay buried? That's what Mack alluded to.

Larry quickly appeared from the hallway beneath the two large staircases. His long bathrobe was open, revealing only a pair of boxer shorts beneath.

"What the hell are you doing here?" he shouted, closing in on my position in a hurry.

"We need to talk. You and I." What we had to talk about was something I hadn't figured out yet.

Larry walked up next to Jon. "What did I tell you about talking to strangers?" He smacked him on the side of the head.

"Don't do that," I said.

"What?" Larry said, taking a step closer to me.

"Don't hit him. Don't you realize all you're doing is passing on that behavior to Jon? Is that what you want him to become? A bully, like you?"

"Fuck you," Larry said. "Who are you to tell me anything? Get the fuck out of my house."

I stood my ground. "No. I'm not leaving."

"Oh, is that right? Why don't you wait here while I go get some persuasion?" Larry began to walk up the stairs to our left.

"You need a gun? Is that it? You going to try to intimidate me like you do to your own son?"

"He's not my blood. Blame his mother for however he turns out."

What a douche. I looked over at Jon. He had his head down. I never thought I'd find myself sticking up for a bully. They did such damage to me growing up that I almost wanted to see a bully get a dose of his own medicine. But Jon was still a kid in my eyes. And his situation was no different than mine. It all came down to power and who wielded it. I would not relinquish mine to Larry.

"How can you say something like that? Wasn't she your wife? Isn't Jon your family?"

"Who the fuck are you? Huh? You know my wife or something? That why you're here?" He moved off the stairs and closed to within five feet of me. "I don't like people in my personal business." He grabbed me by my shirt. "Now why don't you get out of here while you still can?" He pushed me closer to the door.

"Stop it, Larry," Jon said.

Larry stopped pushing me and went for Jon. He grabbed him by his ratty t-shirt. "You're going to pay for that later. We'll make some nice new secrets." Then Larry smiled.

I froze in place. A wave of nausea ran from my scalp to my toes. Memories too deeply buried to ever float to the surface did just that. *Nice new secrets*. Painful memories I forgot existed raced forward in my thoughts; memories I had blocked out so long ago. It was always there, lurking in the furthest recesses of my mind, pushed back where I could never revisit it. I never thought about it. I forced myself to forget. But the phrase "nice new secrets" was the exact one used on me when I was a boy.

"Let him go," I said. The repressed memories brought with them a heap of anger; anger that increased by the second.

"Get out of my house."

"You're sexually abusing Jon, aren't you?" I looked to Jon. "He is, isn't he? That's what you didn't want me to find." It was quite an allegation to make, especially while I was inside this man's home. But I felt it in my bones that this was the case. I knew it because I had been in his shoes before. I understood what kind of secrets were kept by people like him. Secrets that ruined lives.

Jon didn't say no. And that was more of a yes than anything could be. He then started to cry. He sank down to the ground and cowered in a ball.

"How fucking dare you," Larry said.

"No," I said. I don't think I ever felt such rage before. "How dare you. You are a disgusting, lying, nothing of a man. Does it make you feel good taking advantage of Jon? Do you feel powerful? Because you shouldn't."

"Get out of here," Larry said. He pushed me back.

I took a step forward to replace the ground I had just lost. I pushed him back, harder.

"It's people like you that bring such pain into this world." I pushed him again. "It's people like you that ruin lives without any sort of concern for anyone but themselves." And again. "It's people like you that make people like me believe we are at fault. And that's just the way you want it. Treat our lives like they are disposable. Use us like we are less than human. Well, that ends today. No more pain. No more."

Larry looked me straight in the eyes. I could see the hate swirl inside them. But unlike my past, I was not afraid to look back. I wanted to look back. I needed to face Jon's monster, because I needed to face my own. The timid child whose innocence was stolen long before it should have been was ready to take back what people like Larry stole. I was ready to take it back for all of us.

I walked over to Jon. I bent down to my knees in front of his curled-up form. "It will be okay, Jon. I promise you. I won't let him hurt you anymore."

Jon nodded but kept crying. Watching him cry brought back more of what I hoped I'd never remember. I had buried the memories so deeply that it felt like I was reliving them all over again. I was much younger than Jon when it began. A family friend. A few night's babysitting. Secrets paid off with candy and toys. I knew at the time it wasn't right. It didn't feel right. I hated it. But adults can be persuasive when they want. They can tell lies, cover-up things, make a child seem like a liar when it's convenient to do so. And when the pain turned to shame, I hid it, like so much else. But I was done hiding.

The first bullet hit the wall above my head.

I spun around to find Larry with a pistol out in front of him as he hopped down over the final few steps.

"Don't you understand, Sean?" he said. "I am part of who you are. Without me, you will crumble apart."

What did he mean by that?

"Listen. Put down the gun and let's talk about this."

"There's nothing to talk about." His voice changed as he spoke. "You keep meddling in things you shouldn't. You simply do not listen when it benefits you. I warned you to leave it alone. I told you this would not end well for you if you didn't."

That voice. My fear transitioned to depression. The panic attacks I hadn't been having lately slammed back into me. All the positive energy I'd recently found became submerged in inky water.

I tried to move, but I couldn't. As Larry crept closer he shrank in size and width. He became smaller, paler. He morphed into Drake right before my eyes.

It was hard to breath. *Why now*? Everything seemed like it was getting better.

Drake smiled.

"Leave him alone." It was Mack. *Oh, thank you*! He stood by the front door.

I looked over to him. I tried to speak, but couldn't.

"I was expecting you," Drake said. He looked to the gun in his hand, shrugged, and then tossed it to the side. "Come to try and save him, have you?"

"What you are too blind to see," Mack said, "is that he has already saved himself."

I could only assume they were talking about Jon. What must he be thinking about at that moment? Could he see Drake, too? Or did he still look like Larry to his eyes? I turned to look at him, but Jon was gone. Only Drake, Mack, and I remained in the room.

"You can't save what's not worth saving," Drake said.

"You are as wrong as ever. And your days are over," Mack said. "You will do no more harm. Sean has confronted every part of your existence. And although he doesn't understand so yet, he is past your control."

Did Mack just say that I was past his control?

Drake appeared on my right.

"Is he right, Sean? Are you feeling better?" He turned from the sickly Drake to the family friend I hoped to never see again. The one that abused me in ways that infected every cell in my body. The man who in an instant changed me from a happy child to a depressed shell. My skin crawled. "Are you sure this memory does not bother you any longer?" When he spoke, his voice was that of the family friend, the pedophile, the molester, the monster.

I couldn't speak. Even if I could, I didn't know what to say. What the hell was happening to me? This wasn't real. It couldn't be. But yet it was happening. So what did that mean? A sudden, whopping panic attack took control of me. I started to cry, unintentionally. Was this it? Had I finally succumbed to the demons in my head?

"You needn't be afraid any longer, Sean," Mack said. His voice was powerful and reassuring. "His power is given and taken solely by you. You needn't feed his hunger any longer. Free yourself of his lingering presence. Live your life the way it was meant to be lived. Stand up, Sean. Take back what is rightfully yours."

I stood, seemingly against the invisible force that held me down.

The molester stood, too. He sneered at me across his crooked nose. He then looked at Mack. "He will never overcome me. He created me. And now I will linger into eternity. My roots run down to the bedrock. If you pull one, there are a thousand others ready to hold me up." He morphed back into the sickly Drake.

"You can't ignore him, Sean. You need to confront him. Confront it. The life you needed to save was never Jon's, or Jake's, or Isabella's. It was always your own life that needed saving. Save yourself, Sean."

My jaw felt looser. My chest was still tight, like someone was sitting on it. "I can't live like this anymore. Tell me what I have to do."

"Confront Drake. Tell him how you feel. Don't hide who you are."

I turned to Drake. I shook my head. I had no idea what I was supposed to say.

"Listen to your heart, Sean," Mack pleaded. "Say what it is you need to say."

"I don't know what that is?"

"You do, Sean. Ignore everything else."

I looked back at Drake. His crooked smile, his stringy hair, his pale complexion. I don't know exactly when I decided to put reality on hold, but I was pretty sure it was at that moment. Something inside of me began to bloom. Something I hadn't felt in what seemed like forever. I felt in control of my world, my destiny. For the first time in forever, I felt like I wasn't bound to my depression by thick chains.

My depression.

Mack smiled. "Yes, Sean. Now you understand."

I turned to Drake. "Fuck you." I said. "You have no power over me. You're a weak little nothing, preying on the good and leaving nothing but bad. I'd say that I hate you, but doing so would be exactly what you want. Wouldn't it? You want me to hate you. You thrive on it. Well, I won't give that to you any longer. You are nothing to me." I felt beyond reproach at that moment. And it felt really good. "You hear that, Drake, or whatever your name is? I will never acknowledge you again. I refuse to live within your darkness for even a second longer."

Drake's knowing look quickly soured. "You don't know what you're doing," he said. "Without me, you won't be you."

"That's where you're wrong. Without you, I'll finally be able to be me again. It felt like a white hot light of happiness burned inside of me all of a sudden. It was an amazing feeling. "So why don't you go back to whatever dark hole you crept out of, because you're not welcome here any longer."

"Stop it," Drake said, now on his knees, cowering. "You need me."

"The only thing I need from you is to be gone. Now go!" I screamed.

Drake then vanished in a bright flash of light. And when he did, I felt a million pounds lighter.

The walls began to melt in upon themselves. Everything around me swirled and morphed.

I looked to Mack. "What's happening, Mack?"

He simply smiled from ear to ear. "Change, my boy. Change is happening."

36

"Ignore what's going on around you, Sean. Focus on me," Mack said from directly in front of me.

The world swirled in streaks of black and white. This was it, I figured. I had finally stepped over the line. This is what crazy felt like. I feared there was no coming back from what I had become. I had passed insane. Nothing else could explain this. But at the same time, I felt amazingly liberated and lighter than I had ever felt.

"Focus on me," Mack said again. "It's time you know the truth."

I looked away from the swirls, from the tormented screams, from the images that flashed in front of my eyes as if I was inside a giant television screen. Familiar images, scenes, faces all whipped by before vanishing again.

I looked to Mack. "What truth, Mack. What's happening to me?"

"Your rebirth, so to say."

"Please, Mack. No more funny talk. Just give it to me straight."

"Very well, Sean. That day we met on the roof never happened."

"What?"

"I didn't stop you from jumping that day. No one could have."

The swirling stopped and began to bleed down the walls until we were alone in a dark room. I looked back to Mack.

"I'm not in the mood for jokes right now, Mack."

"This is no joke, Sean. You had given up. Your depression beat you."

I couldn't even grasp the thought. It seemed too farfetched and out there to even entertain. But then I remembered feeling as if I had jumped. I knew I felt the cold wind hitting my face and the rain pelting me as I fell. I knew that all along. But how could that be?

"Am I dead?" I feared the answer.

"No," Mack said. "Not yet. This is going to be difficult to understand. Not because you're incapable of doing so, but because it goes against most of what you know to be real. And while I have not been completely honest with you, I have done so to help get you to this point. You need to continue to trust me."

"Why do I need to do that, Mack? You just told me that you've lied to me this entire time."

"Because you and me are the same person, Sean. I am you and you are me." He simply looked at me after saying that like he just told me an email address or a phone number; very matter-of-factly.

"Here I was thinking that I was losing it. You should see a doctor, Mack." I laughed nervously.

"I told you it would be difficult to grasp. You are still holding on to the last thread of who you never wanted to be. Let it go, Sean. Soak in what I have to tell you and thrive from it. Let *us* thrive from it."

"Just spit it out, Mack. Where the hell are we? What's happening to me?"

"You are in the hospital, Sean. You've been in there since the day you jumped."

I struggled. I mean, I really struggled with the lunacy that Mack was spitting out. I was in a hospital? How was that even remotely possible? I'd been going about my life since that day. My experiences, my thoughts, were they all fake?

"This doesn't look like a hospital, Mack." It didn't look like much of anything.

"I assure you that you are in a hospital. And extremely lucky to be alive. Your body is in terrible shape. But your mind is better than it's ever been. My job was to make sure you wanted to live. Because if you didn't, then none of this would be worth it."

"Why would it matter if I wanted to live or not?"

"It's an important distinction, Sean. You've been surviving for the past few years. But you haven't been living. There was no point in fighting against death if you simply wanted to survive."

As crazy as it all sounded, I couldn't help but to feel like Mack was somehow, someway, telling me the truth.

"So where are we now?" I asked.

"You have been in a medically-induced coma. We are in your mind. We have always been in your mind. With my help, a familiar world was created so you could deal with what ailed you."

My mind?

"Yes. Your mind." *How did he know I thought that*?

"Because, like I said, you and me are the same. I am you, you are me. You can think of me as your subconscious. I am the one that pleaded with you not to jump that day. I begged you not to do it. Your mind was too polluted to listen."

"If we are the same person, then why is your name Mack? Why even bother giving you a name?"

"You were on the cusp of a breakdown before you tried to kill yourself. The world we created needed to be real. Mack is the name you subconsciously gave me to help sort through everything. When you leaned off the building, you didn't fall straight down. If you had, we'd be dead. In a strange way, your luck changed the second you committed to ending it all. A few fire escapes and laundry lines broke your bones and your fall, until you fortuitously landed in a large snow pile the city had been building outside the building's entrance. The fact that you survived was a miracle all unto itself."

I felt woozy. I needed to sit. No sooner had I thought it when a chair appeared below me. I sat.

"But why the name Mack? I've never known a Mack in my life."

"My appearance is that of the man who stopped his truck from running you over when your broken body slid down the pile of snow and into the busy street. He drove a large Mack truck. It was the final image you saw before blacking out. And that was when I stepped in.

Or, as you probably remember it, when I showed up on the roof."

"What about everything that has happened since then? Are you telling me that it wasn't real? It never happened?"

"Does the fact that it happened in your mind rather than in the physical world make it any less real?"

"Yes, Mack. That's exactly what I would say. Or whatever your name is. Whoever you are. This is all imagined." Then it occurred to me. "What about Jake? And Isabella? And Jon, and Billy, and Richard, and everyone else I encountered since I jumped. They aren't real either?"

"They were faces for your problems. You needed to fix yourself. And in order to do that, you needed to fix them."

"So, if I'm alive, why am I still in here with you?"

"You need to want to leave. Your newly found desire to live is your key."

My key?

"Yes, Sean," he said, again answering my private thoughts. "Don't dismiss it. Think. Doesn't it seem strange that the people you helped all in some way had similar issues to you? Isabella was a beaten woman like your mother. Jake had a gambling addiction and drowned his sorrows in alcohol. And Jon was abused by his stepfather, and in turn bullied others because of it. Even Richard at the Golden Mug lost the love of his life, just like you did. All of these events, and more subtle ones, were created with the sole intent of getting you past your depression, because your depression manifested itself from these issues. As it grew stronger, the weaker your will became. Now you need to accept it."

My depression?

"Yes," Mack answered again to my own private thoughts. "Stop trying to refute everything. Think, Sean. You already know all of this. You're no longer clouded. You beat it. You beat him."

Him? "You mean Drake, right?" It was becoming clearer. And that scared me more than anything ever had.

Mack nodded. "D for depression. D for Drake. His manifestation was how you envisioned it would look if it was in a physical form. It was your depression that tried to stop you from mending your broken mind. It was your depression that held you up in that convenience store, that made you crash into that tree, and that tried to stop you every step of the way. Your depression wants you to die, Sean. And still, despite everything you have put yourself through, it still has a chance to win. Don't let it win, Sean."

The more he spoke, the number I became. The events since climbing onto the roof all those days back didn't actually happen. I never saved Isabella. I never met Jake. Jon was a figment of my imagination.

"You are not going crazy, Sean." Mack said, answering my unasked thoughts. "You are ready to live. Really live. But you must at all costs accept that your life is worth it. Your depression mustn't be allowed to strangle you that close to death. You created it. And you overcame it. Depression's sole purpose is to blind you to all that is good in your life, make you see nothing but darkness. It succeeded in doing that. But it didn't count on you fighting back. It didn't count on your willingness to *change*."

I reached into my pocket and removed the Zippo. *Change*. I traced the word again, slowly.

Mack looked to it. "That was to remind you when you needed reminding. You haven't been alone on this journey. I've come and gone when I needed to. Sometimes for your own good, other times to help your physical body when it needed it more. Those six weeks you thought you lost were a battle your body needed to fight. There was no time to deal with anything but that. But I've been with you the entire time. I am always with you."

"This is a lot to handle, Mack." That was probably the understatement of the century. I believed him, though. I knew that despite it being one of the craziest things I had ever heard, it was somehow real. "So, what now?" I asked.

"That's up to you," Mack answered.

Then the dark room became a bit lighter. The same dim halo of light that I saw in my nightmares glowed from above us.

"What's happening? Is this the end, Mack?"

He smiled. "No, Sean. This is only the beginning."

The light became brighter. Then I heard the voices again. The same ones from my nightmares. I could understand them now. I heard them as if they were right next to me. I wasn't fearful of hearing them any longer.

"I think he's waking up," one of the women said.

"Get the doctor," another said.

Mack began to fade as the light grew even brighter.

"Mack," I said. "Don't leave."

"Like I said, Sean. I am you, you are me. We are always together. We are one."

"What should I do?" I asked as Mack faded to almost nothing.

"Live, Sean. Make what you just went through worth it."

The blackness vanished, replaced by the glowing halo that I came to quickly see was a circular light over my hospital bed.

I felt someone wrap their arms around me.

"Sean!"

It was Beth, my ex-fiancé. I would know her voice anywhere. She hugged me tightly, careful of the maze of wires that ran all over my body and up into my face. She kissed me on my cheek. I couldn't feel it, as my beard was still where it was when I jumped. My hair was still gangly and unkempt. I had only cut it off in my mind. "I'm so sorry. I didn't know you were going through so much." She began to weep softly. "I'm here for you now."

My legs were both immobile, hanging in casts from an apparatus over my hospital bed. One arm was in traction. I used my other hand, the only part of my body that appeared functional, to reach up and touch her face.

"Don't you dare be sorry," I said. "I needed to go through what I did to be able to see what I had. I've never felt freer. For the first time in a long time, I want to live." And I would never let Drake into my world again.

THE END

www.ingramcontent.com/pod-product-compliance
Lightning Source LLC
La Vergne TN
LVHW050925080826
845145LV00001B/213

* 9 7 8 0 9 9 0 4 8 2 3 3 8 *